Smithy & the Hun by Edgar Wallace

Richard Horatio Edgar Wallace was born on the 1st April 1875 in Greenwich, London. Leaving school at 12 because of truancy, by the age of fifteen he had experience; selling newspapers, as a worker in a rubber factory, as a shoe shop assistant, as a milk delivery boy and as a ship's cook.

By 1894 he was engaged but broke it off to join the Infantry being posted to South Africa. He also changed his name to Edgar Wallace which he took from Lew Wallace, the author of *Ben-Hur*.

In Cape Town in 1898 he met Rudyard Kipling and was inspired to begin writing. His first collection of ballads, *The Mission that Failed!* was enough of a success that in 1899 he paid his way out of the armed forces in order to turn to writing full time.

By 1904 he had completed his first thriller, *The Four Just Men*. Since nobody would publish it he resorted to setting up his own publishing company which he called Tallis Press.

In 1911 his Congolese stories were published in a collection called *Sanders of the River*, which became a bestseller. He also started his own racing papers, *Bibury's* and *R. E. Walton's Weekly*, eventually buying his own racehorses and losing thousands gambling. A life of exceptionally high income was also mirrored with exceptionally large spending and debts.

Wallace now began to take his career as a fiction writer more seriously, signing with Hodder and Stoughton in 1921. He was marketed as the 'King of Thrillers' and they gave him the trademark image of a trilby, a cigarette holder and a yellow Rolls Royce. He was truly prolific, capable not only of producing a 70,000 word novel in three days but of doing three novels in a row in such a manner. It was estimated that by 1928 one in four books being read was written by Wallace, for alongside his famous thrillers he wrote variously in other genres, including science fiction, non-fiction accounts of WWI which amounted to ten volumes and screen plays. Eventually he would reach the remarkable total of 170 novels, 18 stage plays and 957 short stories.

Wallace became chairman of the Press Club which to this day holds an annual Edgar Wallace Award, rewarding 'excellence in writing'.

Diagnosed with diabetes his health deteriorated and he soon entered a coma and died of his condition and double pneumonia on the 7th of February 1932 in North Maple Drive, Beverly Hills. He was buried near his home in England at Chalklands, Bourne End, in Buckinghamshire.

Index of Contents

CHAPTER I

THE MILITARY ANARCHIST

"The worst of being a mug," said Private Smith, "is that you usually look it. That ain't my point of view, an' it's not original, bein' the idea of one of the grandest lawyers that ever went into the Army. This chap's name was Grassy, and he joined our battalion owin' to some trouble he'd had with his girl.

"Offen and offen he's told me an' Nobby the story.

"'It was like this,' he sez. 'Me an' Miss So-an'-so was engaged, an' one night me an' her met at So-an'-so's. I happened to remark so-an'-so, and she up an' said so-an'-so, an' finished up by tellin' me that I was so-an'-so so-an'-so.

"'After them illuminatin' remarks of yourn,' sez Nobby admirin'ly, 'I can't see what else you could have done,' he sez. 'Naturally, after a lady has said so-an'-so to you, there's nothin' left to do but so-an'-so. What's your opinion, Smithy?'

"'So-an'-so,' I sez.

"Grassy never spoke out plain in his life. He was one of those fellers who was always scared of committin' himself, an' was always, so to speak, on his guard against givin' evidence against himself. One day on parade he made the drill instructor very wild.

"'When I say "Right turn," what do I mean?' sez the sergeant.

"'I shouldn't like to say,' sez Grassy—'not,' he sez, 'in the presence of witnesses!'

"That was his game—he was a born lawyer.

"'It's in me blood,' he told me an' Nobby one day in the canteen. 'I can no more help it than a cat can help likin' canaries. Me father was a nusher in a court, an', so to speak, I've imbibed the taste for lawyerin'.'

"'Is it hard to learn?' sez Nobby.

"Grassy shook his head.

"'It would be to you,' he sez, 'but it comes natural to me. It's like this,' he sez. 'Suppose Richard Doe owes five pound to John Roe, an' Richard Doe has give John Roe security for the said amount with a contingency an' Richard Roe can't pay on or about the appointed day, what does John Doe do?'

"'Is that lor?' sez Nobby, very impressed.

"'That's lor,' sez Grassy. 'Now I'll try you with another. A. promises B. a house on condition that C. pays B. what B. owes A.—do you foller me?'

"'No,' sez Nobby. 'But don't let that stop you.'

"When Grassy was pinched by the provost-sergeant for breakin' out of barracks an' brought before the colonel he got ten days' C.B.

"'Pardon me, sir,' sez Grassy; 'on a question of lor—I'd like to point out that the police-sergeant had his badge on the wrong arm, which, in a manner of speakin', invalidates the aforesaid conviction,' he sez.

"The colonel leans back in his chair, sort of weary.

"'Will you take my punishment or be tried by court-martial?' he sez.

"'On a point of lor,' sez Grassy, 'an' in view of the famous precedent of the King v. Cassidy, I'll be tried by court-martial, where,' he sez, 'the wells of justice, sir, will be untainted by the prejudice of caste.'

"So Grassy was tried by court-martial, consistin' of the adjutant, a young lieutenant who was scared of the adjutant and did what he was told, and a chap of the Rifle Brigade, who spent most of the time examinin' the probable starters an' jockeys what he'd got hid in the Manual of Military Law; an' the end of it was that Grassy got fourteen days' cells. He came out of cells a confirmed anarchist.

"One night he came into the canteen, flushed an' happy, as Mr. Garvis, the celebrated poet, sez, an' beckoned me an' Nobby aside.

"'Comrades,' he sez, highly mysterious, 'I've news to impart. We're goin' to abolish war.'

"'That's a very serious thing to do,' sez Nobby. "'What's to become of B Company?'

"'Us an' the Rochester branch,' sez Grassy, takin' no notice of Nobby's remark, 'have passed a resolution an' we're actin' with the Paris an' the Russian an' German branches. War,' sez Grassy, 'is a thing of the past. The moment it's declared me an' 40,000,000 others are goin' on strike. We're goin' to down tools,' he sez.

"'In that case,' sez Nobby, 'I'm sorry for you, Grassy, because it means you are goin' to sacrifice your jaw.'

"Grassy's best pal was a feller named Cheevie. It's difficult to describe Cheevie. He was one of those chaps who looked as though somebody had covered his face with glue and then dipped it in hair. If it was possible to unshave yourself you'd always look like Cheevie. He was a great feller on liberty an' freedom. His idea of liberty was that if a man didn't want to pay his debts hisself nobody had the right to make him. Him and Grassy used to talk by the hour about the Brotherhood of Man, an' how we'd all be a gran' family party if it wasn't for tyrants.

"'Do you know what my idea of a tyrant is?' sez Cheevie, very fierce.

"'Yes,' sez Nobby. 'He's any feller who makes you wash your neck.'

"But it was on the subject of war that Grassy and Cheevie was most talkative.

"'War,' sez Grassy—'horrid war! Raisin' your hydrant head an' squirtin' venom down the grooves of time!'

"'Oh, crool war!' sez Cheevie. 'Never again wilt thy mantle be drawn from the sheath of madness an' flown on the masthead of civilisation's pinnacle.'

"Then one day people began to talk about war with Germany. It came all of a sudden, an' the excitement amongst the peace-lovin' infantry was immense.

"'I don't believe there's goin' to be any war,' sez Grassy; 'but, anyway, at the first outbreak we've made our plans. We're sendin' out 1,000,000 four-page leaflets in English, French, German, Russian, Spanish, Italian, an' Irish,' he sez, 'work will immediately stop, factories will cease to fact, an' collieries will coll no more; but I don't think there'll be any war.'

"That night his pal Cheevie came up to see him in the canteen.

"'What will you do, comrade,' he sez, 'if this accursed war breaks out?'

"'There ain't goin' to be a war,' sez Grassy.

"'But suppose there is—you will lay down your arms?'

"'Naturally, comrade,' sez Grassy.

An' refuse to slay your brothers in Germany?' sez Cheevie.

"'Trust me,' sez Grassy. 'But there ain't goin' to be any war.'

"But one afternoon the news came to barracks. War was as good as certain, an' then the crownin' news of all that the reserves was to be called to the colours an' the Anchesters were warned for active service.

"It was one of them holy an' joyous moments when everybody shook han's with anybody. Provost-corporals shook han's with fellers they'd pinched in the town; even D Company was on speakin' terms with A Company, an' the quarter-master-sergeant was civil to the orderly man.

"Cheevie came into barracks in a state of great excitement. He met me on the square.

"'Where is Comrade Grassy?' he sez. 'Is he under arrest for holdin' them beautiful opinions? Is he in the han's of British military-ism for his true, patriotic action in layin' down his arms? Tell me the worst,' he sez, 'an' the world shall know.'

"'He's in the canteen,' I sez.

"'Ah!' sez Cheevie. 'He's thinkin' things out.'

"'No,' I sez. 'He's drinkin' things in.'

"I followed Cheevie to the canteen. There was ole Grassy, talkin' nineteen to the dozen.

"'Comrade,' sez Cheevie, seizin' him by the hand, 'the blow has fallen, the die is cast away; to your own self be true, as dear old Comrade Shakespeare sez, an' it follers you can't find fault with any other man.'

"'Halloa, Cheevie!' sez Grassy, very cold.

"'Comrade—say, comrade,' sez Cheevie, most earnest, 'what are you goin' to do?'

"'What am I goin' to do?' sez Grassy, amazed. 'Why, I'm goin' on active service,' he sez, very loud, 'accordin' to the lor.'

"'But, comrade,' sez Cheevie, very agitated, 'you ain't going to kill your brother German!'

"Grassy glared at him.

"'Don't you go castin' aspersions on my marksmanship,' he sez, very fierce, 'and don't you call me comrade, me man.'

"'What about your opinions?' sez Cheevie.

They're temp'ary suspended,' sez Grassy, 'under martial law,' he sez, an', turning to the fellers who was standin' round him, he sez: 'As I was saying when this low feller interrupted me, the best way to kill a German is to shoot him in the stomach—'"

CHAPTER II

"I often wonder," said Private Smith, thoughtfully, "if Nosy will come back to what I might term 'the fold' in answer to one of them stirrin' appeals which the taxi-drivers are makin' to their feller-creatures.

"Fellers are joinin' the Army now in a different spirit to what Nosy joined, and, anyway, Nosy's settled down.

"But havin', in a way, the dramatic instinct in his blood, he's just as likely to arrive unexpectedly.

"He was a fattish feller, by the name of Parker—hence the expression 'Nosy'—but in civil life he was called Mister Parker, owin' to his wearin' a watch an' chain an' sleeve-links.

"The first time I met him was at a 'do' given by the Anchester Young Men's Improvement Society. Me an' Nobby was invited, an' a lot more young gentlemen of B Company.

"I got fairly friendly with him, an', like a true friend, he began to lumber his troubles on to me. He was havin' a row with his girl over the question of her mother.

"'She's a bit too sarcastic for me,' he sez. 'The other day when I took a bunch of flowers up to Millicent she up an' asked me why I didn't buy her somethin' she could eat. I won't stand it,' sez Mister Parker; 'for two pins I'd—I'd join the Army.'

"'What!' I sez.

"'I'd go for a soldier,' sez Mister Parker, very desperate; 'that'd bring Millicent to her senses.'

"'It would,' I sez; 'an' you.'

"I don't think he meant what he said at the time, but matters goin' from bad to worse, he got gloomier an' gloomier.

"'The old woman's sarcasticker than ever,' he sez, one night when I met him in the High Street. 'I hinted to her that if things didn't alter I'd go in for a red coat, an' she asked me what the Army had done to deserve it.'

"'She's probably right,' I sez.

"'I've nearly made up my mind,' he sez, shakin' his head warnin'ly; 'it's either suicide or the Army.'

"Try 'em both,' I sez.

"Well, Mister Parker's love affair got worse an' worse, an' it ended up by Millicent walkin' out with another feller, an' the poor young feller—Mister Parker, I mean—got proper brokenhearted.

"An' the very next day, very pale and determined, down he came to barracks an' enlisted.

"Mister Parker's idea was that, havin' taken the step of joinin' the Army, the worst w'as over, an' he was preparin' to sit down an' be comfortably miserable, but, unfortunately, there ain't any arrangements in the Army for brooders.

"'A soldier's life an' a soldier's death is what I want,' sez Mister Parker, sittin' on his bed-cot; when in walked Corporal Jones.

"'Parker?' he sez.

"That's me, me man,' sez Nosy, kindly.

"'Not so much "me man,"' sez the corporal, 'or I'll land you in the cage—you'll be for coal-fatigue.'

"'What's that?' sez Nosy.

"'Carryin' coal,' sez the corporal, 'to the married quarters.'

"'What's it like?' sez Nosy.

"'Very much like carryin' civilian coal,' sez the corporal, 'only it's a bit heavier.'

"What with scrubbin' floors and scrubbin' tables, and doin' other things too numerous an' disgustin' to mention, Nosy began to get an idea of soldierin' that he had never had before. He got into trouble for givin' lip to a sergeant, an' got extra drill for bein' too much of a gentleman to wash his neck on a cold mornin'.

"He hadn't seen Millicent since he enlisted, because, in those days, young recruits weren't served out with their swagger tunics for a month or so after they joined, but when that time came, an' he got his nice fine-cloth coat, he dressed up an' went down town.

"He saw her, and she saw him, an' went past him with her nose in the air, an' poor old Parker was terribly upset when he came back.

"'She must have mistook you for a scarlet-runner,' I sez.

"'No, it ain't that,' he sez, mournful; 'she despises me—I'll try her again.'

"So he did; stopped an' spoke to her, an' the only result was that her mother wrote to the C.O. an' said that if he didn't keep his drummer-boys from following her daughter she'd write to the papers.

"'Drummer-boys!' he sez; 'that shows her sarcastic tongue! Drummer-boys!'

"He was a great schemer, was Nosy Parker, an' he sat down to think of a good way to get the girl to see the kind of hero she was chuckin' away. After thinkin' for three days he struck an idea, an' came to me with it.

"'I'll rescue her,' he sez.

"'From what?' I sez; for now that Nosy's engagement was broken off I couldn't see what there was to be rescued from.

"'From ruffians,' sez Nosy. 'One dark night when she's goin' home from choir practice two fellers will spring out of a dark corner an' pinch her watch. Just as she is strugglin' an' at her last gasp, up comes a gallant young soldier. Who is it? By heavens, 'tis Private Parker! Biff! biff! Smack! smack! Down goes the two ruffians, an' the girl falls faintin' in me arms,' sez Nosy, very breathless.

"'Fine,' I sez; 'but suppose all the biff! biff! is done by the ruffians, an' you fall faintin' in her arms?'

"'That,' sez Nosy, 'I'm goin' to arrange for; in fact, it's what I've come to see you about. Will you be a ruffian?'

"'For how much?' I sez, cautious.

"'For five shillin's,' he sez.

"'I'll think about it,' sez I, an' went off to talk the matter over with Nobby.

"Money was very scarce, an' it was the longest month I'd ever lived, owin' to aforesaid.

"So we collected ten shillin's from Nosy, an' Nosy, who was a bit of a poet, wrote out the part. He wrote it out just as if it'd been a play. He used to write plays for the Anchcster Young Men's Improvement Society till somebody stopped him. The play he wrote for us went like this:—

"Scene—A lonely street, with nobody about except the moon. Enter Millicent, a fair young girl.

"Millicent: Methought I heard the village clock proclaim the hour of half-past eleven. How weary I feel! Would that I had never quarrelled with Hector.

"'Wouldn't it sound better if she said "Nosy"?' I sez.

"'No, it wouldn't,' sez Nosy, short. 'Let's get on.'

"Millicent: Oh! woe the day when a cruel mother tore me from his arms with her sarcastic tongue. But hold! I must away, for the hour waxes late.

"(Enter two ruffians.)

"Oh, heavens! who is this?

"Ruffians: Woman! Stand! Deliver your watch and chain.

"Millicent: Help!

"Ruffians: Thy cries are vain. Hand over the stuff, or we will slit thy pretty throat.

"Millicent: Help! Save me!

"Ruffians (seizing her): There is no one here to help you.

"(Enter Hector.)

"Hector: Yes, I am. (Biff! biff! biff!).

"'Do you think you'll remember it?' sez Nosy, anxious.

"'The only thing I want to know,' sez Nobby, 'is this: do we hit you back?'

No,' sez Nosy.

"'Then I don't take no part in it,' sez Nobby. "But we persuaded him, an' when the night of the performance came round me an' Nobby went up to a little street where Nosy took us, an' waited.

"'She'll be comin' along in about ten minutes,' sez Nosy, all a twitter of excitement. 'I'll be waitin' round the corner. You'll know her by—anyway, I'll give you the tip.'

"Bimeby we got the office from Nosy, who was hidin' round the comer.

"'Here she comes,' he hissed, an' at the other end of the deserted street sure enough she appeared.

"When she got near us I steps up to her.

"'Beg pardon, miss,' I sez; 'have you got the time?'

"'Certainly,' she sez, sweet, an' pulls out her watch.

"'Quarter-past nine,' she sez; then she looks up.

"'You're in the Anchester Regiment, aren't you?'

"'Yes, miss,' I sez.

"'Do you know a young man named Parker?'

"'Know him very well, miss,' I sez.

"'How does he like the new life?' she sez.

"'He loves it,' I sez.

"'He's a very foolish boy,' she sez, with a sigh, 'an' he has made me very unhappy.'

"Just at that minute enter Hector. He came dashin' round the corner.

"'Ruffians,' he sez, 'unhand the lady!'

"He biff-biffed, but I wasn't takin' any.

"'Hold hard!' I sez.

"'Fall down,' he whispers, an' landed Nobby in the jaw.

"Nobby was so surprised that he hit back, an' down went Nosy.

"'Don't hurt him,' sez the poor girl, 'don't hurt him. Don't you know me, Hector?'

"'Ruffians,' sez Nosy, in a dazed kind of way, 'unhand the lady.'

"He was sittin' up rubbin' his head where Nobby hit him.

"'I am free,' sez the girl. 'Hector, be calm, dear—I am with you; nobody shall hurt you.'

"'Release her,' sez Nosy, wanderin' in his mind, 'or by heavens, my trusty bayonet shall find your foul hearts.'

"'The best thing you can do, miss—' sez Nobby, an' she snapped round at him.

"'The best thing you can do,' she flared, 'is to go away before I give you in charge. I never saw a more cowardly thing than to strike a boy when he wasn't looking.'

"'But, miss—' sez poor Nobby, flabbergasted.

"'Go!' she sez, very tragic; 'leave us.'

"Nosy bought his discharge next week, an' before we left Anchester they were married. They didn't invite us to the weddin', so we didn't send 'em a wreath or anythin'. But me an' Nobby bought a card at the stationer's an' sent it to Millicent's mother. It was a nice little card, marked 'With Deepest Sympathy.'"

CHAPTER III

AT MONS

Private Smith came back from Soissons with no more than an earnest surgeon with the smallest spatula from the amputating case could make good.

They took off his little toe, which had been rather messed up by a ricochetting .311 Mauser bullet.

"Funny place to be shot," said Smithy philosophically. "Fellers have been askin' me how it happened, an' what with Nobby Clark sayin' I was standin' on me head shootin' Zeppelins, an' other chaps passin' remarks about the size of me feet, I'm looking forward to the tag—if you'll excuse the foreign expression—when I'm well enough to start conquerin' the world, beginnin' on Spud Murphy, of C Company.

"No, I shan't be decorated." Smithy smiled largely and mysteriously at the long window of the ward. "Decorations are a bit too common in the Anchester Regiment.

"When war was declared, an' all the Reservists who'd gone away years an' years before thankin' God that they'd never see the Army again, started rollin' in, shakin' in their shoes for fear they didn't pass the doctor, Mr. Giddiner started his Sober Soldier League. Me an' Nobby, bein' broke at the time, joined it, for Anchester was a bit dull, what with the 'Globe an' Phoenix' an' 'The Stag's Head' an' all the best houses bein' out of bounds.

"The rough idea of the S.S.L. was that, whatever happened, a soldier should never leave the battlefield for a pub.

"'I can't understand,' sez Mr. Giddiner, 'why only you two gallant soldiers have joined. I thought this movement would have spread like wildfire through the Army; you must help me to spread it!'

"'Trust me,' sez Nobby, very confidential; 'you give me all the tobacco an' flannel shirts an' things you want spread, an' I'll spread 'em.'

"But there was nothin' like that to spread—only Emblems of Purity which Mr. Giddiner had bought by the gross from a snide Brum traveller.

"'Disgustin', I call it,' sez Nobby, as we went back to barracks, 'wasting our time like that—not so much as a bloomin' cigarette picture!'

"But Nobby Clark," said Smithy impressively, "ain't the sort o' man to let anything go to waste.

"It was after Maubeuge an' Cateau an' Cambrai an' all them places o' interest on Trench's tour for Nature Lovin' Infantry that Nobby put it up to me.

"'The way the Kaiser's goin' on,' he sez, 'is simply sickenin'. I'm goin' to sell me Iron Cross of the Second Class and the Third Class—wot I got,' he sez, modest, 'for savin' life before Mons.'

"'Whose life?' asks Spud, very suspicious.

"'My life,' sez Nobby, an' took out o' his pocket a square-lookin' cross with a bit o' blue ribbon attached. 'There it is,' he sez, 'an' without the word o' a lie I picked it up on the battlefield: that cross,' sez Nobby, impressive, 'is one of the grandest army decorations in Germany. Zeppelin's got one, Von What's-his-name's got one, an' the Kaiser's got two—one for his uniform an' one to wear on his pyjamas.'

"'Let's have a dekko,' sez Spud—impressed; but Nobby shook his head an' slipped the medal into his pocket.

"'It's too sacred,' he sez.

"'Do you want to sell it?' sez Spud.

"Nobby hesitated.

"'It don't seem right,' he sez. 'After the war's over that cross will be worth pounds.'

"'I'll give you five for it,' sez Spud.

"'It's worth more than five pounds,' sez Nobby; 'but as you're a friend of mine—'

"'Shillin's—not pounds,' sez Spud, an' after a bit of hagglin' Nobby sold it for seven-an'-fourpence.

"'What's S.S.L. stand for?' asks Spud, examinin' the medal suspicious.

"'S.S.L.,' sez Nobby, very slow, 'S.S.L. is the motto of the German army—"Swank Sauerkraut an' Laager."'

"Well, things went on an' on. We got bucketed from hell to breakfast-time, takin' in Compeigny en route. Here there was a slight scrap which under normal circumstances would have been regarded as bein' slightly inferior to the battle of Waterloo, but which under the new rules was put down as an affair of the ninth class. The Guards' Brigade and a cavalry division got home suddenly, an' came climbin' out of the pit o' war with guns stickin' in their hair an' a limber under each arm. We was on the left of the Guards' Brigade, shootin' what Nobby calls the misguided but barbarous mercenaries of culture, an' we were of the fight, but not in it.

"That night, when we bivouacked, Nobby produces another iron cross.

"'You couldn't have found that,' sez Spud nastily, 'because we ain't seen no Germans nearer than 600 yards.'

"Nobby nodded.

"'You're right,' he sez; 'but me own theory is that it dropped out of a Zeppelin. I bestow it upon you, Spud,' he sez, 'the Iron Cross of the first, second, third and dog-box class,' he sez. 'Down on your knees,' he sez, 'an' return thanks to me an' the Kaiser for this glorious day,' he sez. 'You can have it for a couple o' bob an' a packet o' Stinkadoro Fransaze.'

By the time we got to Paris there was hardly a man in B Company who hadn't got one o' Nobby's Emblems of Purity.

"Then come the affair o' the third, when we stood shrapnel for three hours before we worked to the left, to find the place where He Didn't Want It, an' we got close in with the new bayonet, an' there was work for the Pomeranians.

"B Company came out of it sober, but happy, though there were gaps in the pay roll that makes me sick to think about. We were drawin' off that night when we passed a heap of German dead, an' on the top lay an officer, shot through the heart.

"'What's that?' sez Nobby, an' stooped.

"On his breast, near the collar of his grey tunic, was a little medal—a plain black cross.

"We looked at it, then Nobby looked at me.

"'That's the real Iron Cross,' he sez, very quiet, and, bendin' down, he tore it from its ribbon and thrust it deep under the dead man's tunic out of sight.

"'I wonder why you did that?' I sez a little later.

"'That's me culture,' sez Nobby.

CHAPTER IV

SMITHY ON NEWS

Private Smithy moved his bandaged foot tenderly and cased himself up a little in the invalid chair.

"Another excitin' an' momentous week has passed," he said, "broken only by the low moan of anguish from The Times military correspondent, when he found that the command of the Army had been handed back to young Jack French.

"Another week of patriotic endeavour an' valiant doin's.

'Let me enclose,' writes the Bishop of Old Kent Road, 'a letter I have written to the Archbishop of Canterbury about the war. For weeks,' he sez, 'I've seen other names appearin' in print an' have suffered the tortures of the damned at the thought that perhaps I'd never be able to hike meself into the limelight. An' here I am.—Yours truly,

'O. K. Roadimus.

(Enclosure.)

'My Gracious,—This comes hoping to find you well, as it leaves us all at present. What do you think about askin' the soldiers to give up drink? I think it's a grand idea. I'm havin' special pledges printed, which will be served out with the ammunition an' collected by the ambulance. Drink is a curse. Especially on the battlefield. Look at the Germans!

'Your lovin' little brother in the bonds of holiness,

O. K. Roadimus.'

"By the papers," continued Smithy, "I learn that the operations in the West continue; also in the East.

"The following official communiqué is published by the German headquarters staff:—

'On the right we continue to make progress in all directions with one trifling exception. There is some slight opposition to our advance which will be removed as soon as the Anglo-French army is utterly annihilated.

'In the centre we have nothing to report, except that we are advancing in all directions. We are leading the French to their doom.

'On the left we are advancing in all directions with brief intervals of standing still.

'The following news is published by authority:—

London is still in the hands of the hostile Suffragettes an' the Bank of England, which stan's on the Thames Embankment, has been swept by the sea.

Sir Keir Hardie has been made an honorary member of the House of Lords.

An enthusiastic anti-war meetin' was broken up by the brutal police, both members of the audience bein' arrested.

We have again made a successful attack on the "Iron Duke" and captured the crew whilst it was engaged in ironin' its trousers. This brings our list of prisoners up to three million an' six.'

"What is termed the German Lie Factory," continued Smithy, "is workin' shifts. Day an' night the magnificent buildin' is a scene of feverish activity. Its great, great chimnies belch smoke an' sparks an' the thunderin' engines revolve with masterly precision. On the other side of the street is the Iron Cross works. Outside great queues of men are waitin' their turn to be served. There's von Hoppett, of the Intelligence Department, who got two Iron Crosses for agreein' with the Kaiser that it was a fine day; there's von Whoizitt, who got six for heroicly destroyin' a platoon of boy scouts. There's Admiral Salz-Sedletz, who wears Iron Crosses to fasten his braces on.

"Orders are pourin' in; never has iron been so cheap.

"But, despite—if I may be allowed to use the expression—despite, or in spite of the false gaiety of Unter den Linden, the Kaiser has his troubles.

"Twenty-six of his sons are lyin' dangerously wounded, and the Empress is sittin' by their bedsides in Damsick, Poser, Berlin, Munich, Aches, Busseloff, Dresden, Humbug, an' other celebrated places.

"Twenty-eight have lost their legs, an' the Kaiser himself fell in a ditch and contracted congestion of the lung, as a result of which he is now commandin' the army in Eastern Prussia.

"The Serbian Army is now at Itchski—a bit of news which brings relief to thousands of throbbin' hearts that thought it was at Bobrinski —an' the significance of the news that the Drina is still runnin' cannot fail to awake a responsive thrill in British bosoms."

Smithy scratched his nose thoughtfully.

"I've asked to be discharged from hospital," he said. "Me nerves are gettin' a bit fretted with the war in London—I sigh, so to speak, for the peace an' quiet of the River Aisne."

CHAPTER V

ON THE LAWYER IN WAR

"What I like," said Smithy, "is the gallant way the brave lawyers of England have rallied to the colours. It's one of the grandest things we've seen in the war. Many a noble barrister has handed over his important cases at the local County Court an' flocked to the War Office to conduct the campaign.

"Gen'ral McKenna, one of the celebrated lawyers of the age, has put all the lights of London out.

"'In re Zeppelins,' he sez, that bein' the way lawyers talk. 'In re Zeppelins v. Another (me being the another), it is ordered that the action stand over to the Hilarious Term, both sides to pay costs!'

"Every night, surrounded by his gallant staff, the brave gen'ral rides round London lookin' for people who strike matches in the street to the common danger. He rules with an iron hand, his iron heel grinds opposition, his iron heart never quails as his iron eyes sweep the skies for signs of aeroplanes. Everything about him is iron—except his head, an' that's the same old lump o' stuff that floats.

"Lieutenant (temp'ry Colonel) Buckmaster, k.c., is holdin' the Press Bureau to the last nib against the enemy, that has caught more recruits than the finest bunch of lawyers that ever got into fat jobs for the askin'.

"Day by day the defender of Fort Inkpot issues his cheering report:—

On our left a heavy attack by The Times was beaten off with loss. The enemy opened a heavy fire with their famous Remington rifles.

In the action the Globe brought its Naval Brigade into action. We lost one admiral.

On the right a mixed brigade delivered several damagin' sneers at our position, but they made no charge.

To sum up: our position is favourable but unhappy.

"The advantage of havin' lawyers in charge is that they take no risks. They never do anything that ain't in the book.

"Suppose the Germans come to England, an' Field-Marshal Haldane was in charge?

"'Me lud,' sez Colonel Buckmaster, 'the defendants have committed contempt of court by shellin' Buckin'ham Palace.'

"'Order out the heavy battery of Mandamuses,' sez the Field-Marshal firmly; 'deploy the 1st Royal Injunctions an' fight to the last man.'

"'Pardon, me lud,' sez Colonel Buckmaster, 'but in the case of Napoleon versus Wellin'ton it was laid down by Lord Chief Justice Nelson that Mandamuses shouldn't be brought into action until the Injunction had been thrown out of court.'

"The Field-Marshal looks grave.

"'Empanel a jury,' he sez. 'Bring me Chitty on Contracts an' the Army List—send McKenna to turn the lights out, an' give the enemy copies of my celebrated book, Rot mit Uns, to read whilst we get out a written judgment.'

"They're great believers in words," said the admiring Smithy. "They don't do anything till they're told. They had to be told to get bands to help recruitin', they had to be told that Zeppelins couldn't live in a ninety-mile-an-hour gale, they had to be told that the Germans had big guns. The only things they don't believe is they've no what I might term aptitude for conductin' war—an' that's the thing that everybody is tellin' em.

"In a sense I don't blame 'em," Smithy went on. "If you believed everything you was told it would be ridiculous goin' on with the war.

"Have you heard about the Kaiser bein' captured an' brought to England? Do you know that French an' Joffre are one an' the same person—'ence the expression 'French'! Do you know that the Gran' Duke What's-his-name of Russia an' the Kaiser are as thick as thieves? Are you aware that the King of the Belgians an' Colonel Seely are livin' at Harrogate? You haven't? Don't you go to your club?

"I've heard more things in the strictest confidence since the war started than I've heard for donkey's years.

"People are always comin' up to me most mysterious an' tellin' me what Kitchener told a friend of theirs.

"Confidence an' the Press Bureau are the two things you're allowed to abuse in these days.

"These are wonderful times," continued Smithy, shaking his head with melancholy pleasure. "Never before has what I might term the People got so into the ribs of the Government that it can hear the great heart of the Cabinet throbbin' like a B.M.C. taxi.

"Secrets what in peace time would never get known are now handed out with the change. The newspaper boy in the street gives you your Star an' the latest gossip from York Cottage; the feller that cuts your hair can point out the very winder to the Tower where little Prince Looie was smothered by wicked Uncle Winston; an' even the 91st Royal Hoxton (Mike Cassidy's Own) use the time they're not drillin' between school-hours to hold councils of war an' discuss the marvellous way Douglas Haig has got on without influence.

"There was a feller in ours named Anthony Gerrard, who got well thought of by bein' mysterious. He never mentioned names—just like the War Office—preferrin' the use of the alphabet.

"Nobby used to say he got his name out of a telephone book, but Anthony Gerrard, Esq.—that's how he used to sign his name before he enlisted—said he scorned Nobby.

"'There's a certain Lord X.,' sez Tony one night in the canteen; 'I won't give you his name. But suppose I walked up to him an' offered him me hand—what do you suppose he'd do?'

"'Call the police?' sez Nobby.

"'No,' sez Tony, smilin' pityin'ly; 'he'd stagger back an' say: "Good heavens—is it J—"'

"'You bein' the Jay?' sez Nobby.

"'Me bein' J,' sez Tony.

"So long as a feller doesn't commit the error of givin' particulars, he can go on makin' impressions an' giving you the idea that he's in the brightest an' best class, an' that's what Tony did.

"It was a bit sickenin', because when Tony was around you couldn't talk about anybody.

"If somebody started 'They tell me that the Duke of Claremarket—' Tony would cough warnin'ly.

"'I'm here,' he'd say.

"Or suppose somebody started criticism' Balfour, Tony would stop it at once.

"'There's certain reasons,' he'd say, 'why I'd rather you didn't mention Mr. B. Certain family reasons,' an' naturally that would dry us up.

"Nobby was arguin' once about Napoleon Bonaparte. Not exactly arguin', but tellin' a feller that if he said so-and-so he was a liar. Nobby knows a lot about Napoleon, owin' to havin' read a book called The Heroic Drummer Boy, or How England was Saved; A Tale of the Peninsular War.'

"Nobby was in the act of tellin' the chaps how Napoleon used to go round pinchin' people's ears, an' anythin' else he could lay his hand on, when Tony, who was drinkin' solitary at the bar, an' listenin' with a very moody face, steps in.

"'Nobby,' he sez in a pained voice, 'don't think me foolish, but for certain reasons I'd rather you didn't mention N.B.'

"'For why?' sez Nobby.

"'I can't explain,' sez Tony, sorrorful; 'it would mean givin' away certain secrets that have been in the family for years. All that I'll say,' he sez, 'is this: Do you notice anythin' strange about me face?'

"'Yes,' sez Nobby.

"'I don't mean that,' sez Tony, hasty, 'but do you recall a certain resemblance to anybody you've heard about?'

"Nobby suggested a few people, but somehow didn't quite hit the idea.

"'You needn't be offensive,' sez Tony; 'amongst gentlemen there's no need to be rude an' personal. I asked you a civil question. Don't I remind you in some ways of N.B.?'

"'No,' sez Nobby.

"'Well,' sez Tony, drinkin' up his beer, 'we won't go into the question, but it's very painful for me to stand here an' listen to certain things said about certain people.' An' with that he walks out.

"It was about this time that Tony began to take up his family as a serious hobby. Previous to this, he'd only dropped hints at one time an' another, but now he began to work overtime on the job. He got gloomier an' gloomier; didn't talk much; used to sit in a corner of the canteen nursin' an unsociable pint o' beer, an' broodin'.

"It got to be the talk of the camp. Fellers from other regiments used to come over to our canteen to have a look at him. It got about that he was a German Prince who'd been disappointed in love. Somebody told Tony this an' he denied it.

"'I don't mind admittin',' he sez, 'that I'm not a German Prince. Not German,' he sez, 'at any rate.'

"In order to spare his feelin's, we had to wait until he'd left the canteen before we started an argument about any feller.

"If he happened to be present one of the chaps would go up to him an' say: 'Excuse me, Tony, have you any objection to us discussin' the Kaiser—or Richard Cure de Lions,' as the case might be.

"Sometimes Tony would say 'Yes,' but more often—especially the day we was arguin' about Moses an' the Bulrushes, an' how Moses got there—he said 'No,' he'd rather we didn't.

"Now, all this went on for months. We was shifted from Aldershot to Chatham, an' back again to Aldershot, and as far as me an' Nobby was concerned, we got a bit fed up with Tony an' his family pride.

"Nobby an' me went on leave to London, an' the night after we came back, we was sittin' in the library, so called because it's the only place you can get a cup of coffee, tellin' the other fullers all about our adventures, when in walks Tony, an' I could see the light of battle in his eye, to use a poetical expression.

"I was just in the middle of tellin' the fellers about a certain party me an' Nobby had seen—'The Marvellous Binko' he was called—when in rushed Tony, where a good many other fellers wouldn't have dared trod.

"'Pardon me,' he sez, 'the party you mentioned as I come in is on the stage, ain't he?'

"'He is,' I sez.

"'A short, stout party?' sez Tony, guessin' 'very' hard.

"'He is,' I sez.

"'Well,' sez Tony, 'all I can say is that when a member of a certain family disgraces hisself by goin' on the stage, it don't seem to me that it's a very friendly thing to chuck it in the teeth of another member of the same family.'

"'Meanin' you?' I sez.

"'Yes,' sez Tony, as bold as brass, 'if you're cad enough to make me confess it, yes!'

"'Is "The Marvellous Binko" a member of your family?' I sez.

"'I don't mind tellin' you in confidence that he's me half-brother,' sez Tony, 'an' all our family's very much upset about his goin' on the stage. I've done me best to persuade him not to,' sez Tony, despairin'ly. 'I've argued with him and talked to him. "Think o' the family," I sez, but he took no notice.'

"'Shouldn't think he would,' I sez, 'because the party me an' Nobby was talkin' about is the Educated Chimpanzee at the Palace. I tell you this,' I sez, 'in the strictest confidence!'"

CHAPTER VI

VON KLUCK'S NEPHEW, GINGER

"Talkin' as I was last week," said Smithy, "about people with relations reminds me of von Kluck's nephew, what we discovered in the course of a slight argument about Napoleon an' the Kaiser.

"The main difference between the Kaiser and Napoleon Bonaparte," said Smithy, "is that Napoleon is dead an' respected an' the Kaiser is alive.

"Other differences don't count. Everybody knows that Napoleon never 'made satisfactory progress'—he won. Everybody knows that Napoleon wasn't much of a speech maker, an' everybody knows that when he gave out the Iron Crosses of the period, so to speak, the fellers who got 'em had to earn 'em.

"When we was marchin' down to the Marne there was, as I say, a great argument—after we got our second wind—as to whether Napoleon was a better gen'ral than von Kluck.

"The only feller that stuck out for von Kluck was a red-haired chap named Ginger. Ginger had an aunt who ran away from home when she was a girl, an' disgraced the family by marrying a German by the name of Kluck, an' Ginger always spoke of von Kluck as 'Uncle Hector.'

"'It's my belief,' sez Nobby, 'that you're a spy, Ginger, an' you ought to be shot.'

"'That's no argument,' sez Ginger; 'an' if it comes to shootin', I can only hope that the firin' party will be rotten third-class shots like you.'

"'If,' sez Nobby, taking a long breath, 'if I wasn't on active service fightin' for me country,' he sez, 'I'd take them remarks of yours an' ram 'em down your throat with me entrenchin' tool.'

"'Don't lose your temper, Private Clark,' sez Ginger—he was a thin, tall feller, with a weary habit of speakin'. 'My Uncle Hector never loses his temper, an' that's why he's pushin' the British Army all over the shop. Now, Napoleon was always losin' his temper, an' spent all his life pinchin' corporals' ears, by all accounts. My Uncle Hector don't pinch ears.'

"'Your Uncle Hector,' sez Nobby, highly exasperated, 'would pinch the bones out of a kipper.'

"'If ever I'm took prisoner,' sez Ginger, musin'ly, 'I'll go straight up to the General an' say: "Hullo—how's Aunt Emma?" I'll bet he'll be surprised.'

"'If he ain't,' sez Nobby, 'he'll come out of this war alive.'

"Ginger had started by wonderin' if von Kluck was a distant relation, and sort of strengthened his the'ries, to such an extent that by the time we started comin' back he knew von Kluck better than he knew the holes in his shirt.

"'Often,' sez Ginger, 'he used to come an' see us down in Deptford. He'd pop over from Germany in his private clothes an' look in for Sunday dinner.'

"'What?' sez Nobby, incredulous, 'does he eat rabbit, too?'

"'My Uncle Hector would eat anything,' sez Ginger, enthusiastic; 'he's one of them hard Germans what you hear about that eats iron filin's.' An' Ginger went on to describe how Uncle Hector would nurse the children an' take his mother out walkin' in Greenwich Park, an' pay for tea like a real gentleman.

"This went on for a long time—in fact, till we got half-way back to the Marne.

"There was a counter-attack made by the Germans. They came into action like a regiment of soldiers, with colours flyin' an' bands playin', an' after the attack had been boiled an' bottled the rumour went along the lines that von Kluck had been taken prisoner. Nobody knows how rumours like that get goin', but there it was, an' Ginger was all a-twitter with excitement. Our company was told off to take the prisoners back to the base—there was about 400 of 'em—an' to make matters more interestin', we was told that there was a German gen'ral amongst 'em who was not to be mentioned.

"'It's 'im,' whispers Ginger, agitated, 'Uncle Hector!'

"We got back to the base, an' all the way down Ginger was castin' his lamps over the crush. There was one feller who didn't walk amongst the prisoners. His uniform was different, an' he had cords an' lacin's all over his tunic.

"'That's him,' whispered Ginger to me; 'I'd know him anywhere—often I've sat on his knee—'

"'Shut your big mouth, Ginger,' sez the corporal of our section, very kindly; 'give the aviators a chance—you're upsettin' the aeroplanes, you windy devil.'

"But just before we handed over our little lot Ginger had a chance. There was a German prisoner who spoke English, an' Ginger asked him, very mysterious:

"'Is there a feller named Kluck here?' he sez.

"'That's him,' sez the low Hun, and pointed to the distinguished-lookin' feller with the cords on his chest.

"I don't know what made Ginger do it, because nobody had bet him that he wouldn't, but he ups an' walks to the big chap an' holds out his hand.

"'Hullo, Uncle Hector,' he sez.

"The big feller louks at him, very surprised.

"'You're Kluck, ain't you?' sez Ginger, an' the big feller nods. 'Well,' sez Ginger, all of a tremble, 'I'm Fred,' he sez; 'don't you remember playing with me, Uncle Hector?'

"The big chap shook his head,

"'Mit you—no,' he sez, 'vor you—yis, perhaps. I am der big trommer of the Vorty-eight Jaegers,' he sez."

CHAPTER VII

ON MEANING WELL

"Nothin'," said Private Smith, "succeeds in this world like knowin' what you want an' sendin' in somebody else to get it. Another grand way of gettin' on, especially in the lit'ry line, is to go out for things that nobody else wants an' pretendin' it's the only real goods in the market. Look at Bernard Shaw, the celebrated poet.

"There wasn't a day passed before the war but he wasn't tellin' unpleasant truths that nobody ever thought of tellin', because from their point of view they was lies.

"That's why I think we're wrong about Germany. They're tellin' the truth—from their point of view.

"When they burn down a cathedral they can prove that they're lendin' a helpin' hand to civilisation.

"'Hullo,' sez the Kaiser, 'what's this on the horizon?—Reims Cathedral or a picture palace?'"

"'That, your worshipful Magesty, amen,' sez von Kluck, 'is the cathedral.'

"'Shell it,' sez the Kaiser, 'in the name of Kultur,' he sez, 'to encourage the poor bricklayers' labourers of France,' he sez. 'Hand me the unemployed returns of France which our head spy cut out of the Daily Way,' he sez.

"'Yes, Almighty-for-Ever-an'-Ever,' sez von Kluck, an' takin' a gilt-edged bit of the Daily Way out of his diamon'-covered satchel, he passes it to the Kaiser, an' the Kaiser has a dekko.

"'As I thought,' he sez, 'masons and bricklayers are unemployed—shell it,' he sez, 'in the name of humanity.'

"An' it was similar with Louvain.

"'What's the name of this place?' sez the Kaiser.

"'Holy sir,' sez von Kluck, 'the name at the railway station is Louvain.'

"'So!' sez the Kaiser bitterly, 'this is the place where all them old-fashioned authors is patronised,' he sez, 'whilst up-to-date fellers like Charles Garvice an' Hall Caine an' Edgar Wallace is starvin' on half salary—we will have a wave of progress,' he sez, 'a heat wave.'

"There was a feller of ours by the name of Gumbal—we used to call him Gumboil for short—who was always doin' things with a good object.

If you missed your blackin' brush an' searched his kit an' found it, he'd explain how he was doin' you a turn.

"'If it hadn't been for me,' he sez to Nobby very indignant, 'you'd have lost that pair of boots—I saw 'em kicking about an' took care of 'em.'

"'The nex' time you see 'em kickin' about,' sez Nobby very unpleasant, 'you sit down quick, because my feet'll be inside 'em.'

"Gumboil's habit of explaining away things got him into trouble at Mons. At the height of the attack he had a feelin' that he'd like to go away to somewhere quiet an' lonely to think.

"I've had the feelin' myself, so I don't blame him.

"He got up slowly an' was walkin' away in a dazed kind of manner when his officer called him.

"'Where are you goin'?'

"'Ammunition's run out, sir,' sez Gumboil prompt.

"It so happened that our section was runnin' short, an' the feller whose job it was to bring it up had been wounded.

"'You can't go yet,' sez the officer, 'the ground is swept by the enemy's fire.'

"'I don't mind, sir,' sez Gumboil.

"'Try it,' sez the officer, an' off Gumboil went, across a bit of ground where if he'd been any good to anybody he'd have been killed six times over before he got twenty yards. Bein' naturally awkward an' useless, he got to the ammunition wagon. They loaded him up, an', like a man in a dream, he walked back to the trenches an' distributed the ammunition.

"'You're a brave feller,' sez the officer admiringly, 'an' you can go again.'

"An' all that afternoon poor old Gumboil spent goin' backward an' forward across a bit of field that was so swept with maxim an' shrapnel an' Mauser bullets that you could hardly see across it.

"The next day, as we was edging past Mauberge, pore old Gumboil sez to me:

"'Smithy,' he sez, 'never explain away mistakes,' he sez, 'or you'll have to go on makin' the same mistake for ever. If the worst comes to the worst, say that you meant well.'

"To say that a chap 'means well' is to say that he's a fool. There's always more well-meanin' people in a country than them that don't mean well—the bad-meaners live in Park Lane an' drive home in gilt-edge motor-cars, an' the well-meaners go by Tube. You never hear tell of French or Joffre meanin' well, because they don't.

"Sometimes fellers will come a howler because their best is everybody else's worst.

"It was the time when the regiment was stationed at Borden Camp, an' we was tempor'ily under the command of a new Colonel, who came from another regiment, an' had an idea that he'd only come to the Anchesters just in time to save 'em from being disbanded.

"It was Nobby who found out that the Colonel was mad about botany. He discovered in a book called Who's Which that the Colonel's recreation was botany an' geology, an' that his telephone number was 978416 Mayfly.

"So Nobby started his botany club. You had to pay tuppence a month to the committee, an' every week Nobby an' his club used to go out on a ramble with a book on botany an' a coke hammer.

"You wouldn't think a full-grown Lieutenant-Colonel would be taken in by that kind of guff, but he was, an' the members of the club got all the afternoon passes they required.

"The club used to march out of barracks very solemn an' stately with Nobby at the head—we didn't allow non-coms, to be members—an' when we got a good way from barracks Nobby used to deliver his address.

"'To-day,' he sez, 'we'll study the habits of the famous Red Dande-Lion.'

"'I don't like the beer there, Nobby,' sez one botanist. 'Why not go on to the White Hart?'

"'Hear, hear,' sez the other students.

"'I'm the committee of this club,' sez Nobby sternly, 'an we'll go to the Red Lion. Besides, I've complained to the landlord, an he's having a special brew for us.'

"One day when we was comin' back to barracks we met the Colonel.

"'Well, men,' he sez, 'I'm glad to see you returnin' from your healthy pursuits. What have you been after to-day?'

"'Dandelions, sir,' sez Nobby.

"'Ah! Excellent!' sez the Colonel. 'And—what is the matter with Private Murphy?'

"'A touch of sunstroke, sir,' sez Nobby hastily; 'he was stoopin' to kiss a dandelion, an' the sun got him at the back of the neck—that's why he's singin', sir.'

"The Colonel looks at Spud very suspicious.

"'He hasn't been drinkin', has he?' he sez.

"'Oh, no, sir,' sez Nobby, shocked; 'it's dandelions, sir—the smell of 'em gets into your head.'

"'That's a very interestin' discovery,' sez the Colonel.

"He left us soon after, an' the next time Nobby went up to the Adjutant with a club pass for signature the Adjutant tore it up.

"'If you want to drink,' he sez, 'go to the canteen; our dandelions are as good as the Red Dande-Lions, an' they're cheaper.'

"The Adjutant of the Anchesters was always a bad-meaner.

"Lots of people get the reputation of bein' well-meaners, because they do the right thing at the wrong time.

"Generals don't get up in a cinema theatre and criticise battle-films, an' acrobatic families on their way to the theatre don't find funny ways of crossin' the road. Similarly, it ain't good policy for officers to stick their noses into soldiers' business, except in regulation hours.

"For instance, there never was any good feelin' between us an' the Wigshires, owin' to a little trouble over the rotten way they kept kickin' the ball out of touch in the Army Cup semi-final of '93, when they was one goal up an' there was two minutes to play.

"This was followed by some slight unpleasantness at Aldershot, where one of the Wigs hit one of our chaps over the head with a bed-leg.

"We always had the good luck to be brigaded away from 'em, until three years ago, when we went on manœuvres together, an' then, as luck would have it, we lay side by side in camp.

"The Brigadier was one of them fellers who are always openin' soldiers' homes an' raisin' money for memorial tablets, an' he'd gone through life under the delusion that one regiment was as good as another, an' that the Army was a great happy family where every soldier loved his comrade, an' two British regiments was alike as two Army overcoats.

"Someone must have told him that there was bad blood between the Anchesters an' the Wigshires, an' he organised a Gran' Camp-fire Concert for the two regiments, with the object of promoting brotherly feelin'.

"'I shall go,' sez Nobby; 'I ain't seen bloodshed for years.'

"It appears that there was a feller in the regiment who was known as the Rudyard Kiplin' of the Wigshires owin' to his habit of puttin' bits in the papers, an' before he went over into the Wigshire lines it leaked out that he was goin' to recite a poem called 'The Brave Anchesters, an' how the Wigshires saved them at Klip Drift.'

"Now, everybody knows that at that historic battle the Wigs was only saved from decimation, annihilation, destruction, and other happenin's too numerous to mention by the gallant an' heroic action of B Company, Anchester Regiment—and especially of me an' Nobby Clark.

"'There's goin' to be trouble,' sez Nobby, when we got to the place where the concert was.

"A chap named Nosey, who was a sort of master of ceremonies, showed us the way to a seat near the fire.

"'I trust you men will enjoy yourselves,' he sez; 'me bein' the middle-weight champion of the Brigade, I was hopin' to entertain you with a boxin' exhibition, but there's nobody can stand up to me!'

"'We're bearin' the loss very well,' sez Nobby.

"'You've heard about me, I suppose?' sez Nosey.

"'I never read the police news, meself,' sez Nobby.

"'You're not tryin' to insult me, are you?' sez Nosey very fierce.

"'Not noticeably,' sez Nobby.

"The real trouble didn't start till Rudyard II started his poem. It began:

'Oh, list, ye gallant Wigshires,
I will a tale relate,
About our glorious regiment,
That's very up to date.'

"''Ear, 'ear,' sez Nobby, an' the feller went on about the bloomin' 'crush'till me an' the other fellers was nearly ill. Then came the wicked bit.

'The shot an' shell is fallin';
We see the Boers attack.
By heaven, 'tis the Anchesters
That start a-fallin' back!'

"'On a point of order!' sez Nobby, risin', 'I should like to state, on behalf of me gallant comrades, that that statement is a lie.'

"'Order, order!' sez the Wigshires, very indignant, an' the poet proceeded:

'They were too weak to vanquish
The foemen at their front.
It was the gallant Wigshires
That bore the battle brunt.'

"'That's another lie,' sez Nobby loudly.

"He looked round quick. Somebody must have given the officers the tip not to come, for there was none present.

"'It's a lie,' sez Nobby again, an' Nosey stepped forward to do a bit of chuckin' out....

"It took the 1st Royal Scots an' the 2nd West Kents the whole of that night to get us sorted out.

"There was two whitewashed lines laid down between the two regiments," said Smithy, "just the same as you see on a tennis-court, an' the Army Act, King's Regulations, an' other deadly military instruments was used an' employed, so to speak, to prevent any further scenes of indescribable disorder.

"Any feller of the Wigshires or Anchesters who put his foot over his own frontier was liable to death or any less punishment as is in this Act mentioned. The papers had somethin' about 'disgraceful military riot,' but as me an' Nobby gave up readin' newspapers, owin' to none of their tips comin' off, it didn't worry us.

"But Nosey did.

"He gave himself out as the middle-weight champion of the Brigade, an' offered to fight Nobby for the Honour of the Regiment an' five shillin's.

"'If I thought he had five shillin's,' said Nobby, 'I'd go into the enemy's country an' do great execution.'

"Receivin' no answer to his challenge, Nosey sent a spy into our camp by night, an' left an insultin' message pinned on to the flap of Nobby's tent.

"An' every day Nosey an' his pals would come down to their line an' shout things that'd make your flesh creep.

"We'd have gone over an' cleared 'em out, but the Adjutant got wind of the idea, an' paraded B Company.

"'There's a court-martial for any of you fellers that cross that line,' he sez.

"'Beg pardon, sir,' sez Nobby, 'but they're always throwin' notes over the line challengin' us to fight. What can we do?'

"'I'll speak to the Colonel of the Wigshires about it,' sez the Adjutant; 'but I don't mind you throwin' messages back, so long as they're civil.'

"That afternoon Nosey chucked over a letter:

'Will you fite me? Yes or no? Will call for arnser at 6.'

"Me an' Nobby spent all the afternoon writin' the answer.... No, it wasn't a long one, just the simple word 'Yes'; but it took us a long time, because Nobby an' me chiselled it on to a bit of pavin' stone, an' when Nosey called for his answer he got it—in the neck."

CHAPTER VIII

THE PERSEVERING SOLDIER

"There's grand news from Germany in the paper this morning," said Private Smith.

'On the East we're makin' progress an' steadily fallin' back in order to deceive the enemy.

'On the South we're advancin' to the rear by short, sharp rushes.

'On the West we're holdin' our own and lots of loot belongin' to other people.

'To sum up, our position is distinctly favourable from a certain point of view, which isn't necessarily ours.'

"Varyin' these with highly confident reports, such as, 'We are winnin' all along the line,' whenever they've got nothin' better to say, the Great General Staff—it sounds like a new omnibus company— manages to give a lot of happiness to people who, in the ordinary course of events, ain't very keen on fiction.

"Perseverance and cocksureness is all very well in its way, an' sometimes it succeeds. Sometimes it only looks as if it succeeds, as in the case of a feller of ours named Chooper. He was a very cocksure feller, an' there wasn't a single thing he wasn't certain about. He knew what kind of weather it was goin' to be; he knew who won the Boat Race in 1644; he knew who Tichborne was, an' why. He was a surprisin' feller. He was like a book of reference, full of printer's errors. He was cocksure about the Army.

"When he enlisted he went down to the tailor's shop to be fitted for his uniform.

"'Halloa!' he sez, when they served him out with his uniform. 'Where's the stripes?'

"'What stripes?' sez the master tailor.

"'Them stripes that the chap wore who enlisted me,' sez Chooper.

"'You fathead!' sez the tailor. 'They was sergeant's stripes. You don't get them till you're promoted.'

"'Then all I can say,' sez the feller, very melancholy, 'is that if I'd known I wouldn't have joined. It's a swindle.'

"Bein' so certain, he was easy money for some fellers"—Smithy coughed—"because the only thing you had to do was to go contrary to his opinions and he'd bet you.

"He was a great feller for jumpin' at conclusions.

"'Commandin' officer's parade is postponed,' he sez one mornin', just before parade, an' the glad news spread.

"'Yes,' he sez, an' began unstrapping the equipment that had took him three hours to put together the day before. 'I saw the Colonel talkin' to the adjutant, an' I heard him say that to-morrow would be a better day.'

"He'd got all his kit to pieces when the 'Quarter' bugle went; he was workin' like blazes to strap up his valise when the 'Fall in' went, and he got seven days for bein' absent from parade in consequence.

"Little things like that would have upset an ordinary man, but this feller wasn't put out in the slightest.

"I used to think that there wasn't anythin' in sanguineness, owin' to my experience with father and with this chap of ours; but I've changed my opinion a bit, because I've seen that bein' stone certain ain't such a bad game as it looks.

"We was stationed in Aldershot when I changed my opinion, owin' to certain things that happened to Chooper.

"Aldershot ain't the bad place that some people think it is. For one thing, there's a decent canal where chaps can go boatin', and it was on one of our trips up to Frimley that Chooper saw a girl on the towin'-path. He looked at her; she looked at him.

"'That girl wants to make me acquaintance,' sez Chooper.

"'A slight mistake,' I sez.

"'Didn't you see her smile?' he sez.

"'I saw her make a face,' I sez.

"'I'll come back here at the same time tomorrow,' sez Chooper. 'She'll be waitin' for me.'

"Now, the surprisin' thing was that when we rowed past the place the next day, there she was (a nice, pretty girl, too), standin' on the bank. She was one of those big, strong girls you see sometimes, and she could have eaten Chooper, who was a little feller.

"We'd have rowed on, but Chooper was steersman, so we pulled into the bank.

"'Good evening,' he sez, and she stared at him. 'I think you've seen me before,' sez Chooper.

"'I don't remember ever seein' a face like yours,' she sez, 'except in the comic papers.'

"This would have put end-of-message to anybody but this feller.

"'My name's Chooper,' he sez.

"'I'm sorry for you,' she sez kindly; 'but we've all got our burdens.'

"'Chooper,' he sez. 'We descended from the Dutch.'

"'It's very interesting,' sez the girl. 'When are you goin' to pick yourself up again?'

"'I see you're busy,' sez Chooper, who wasn't a bit put out. 'I'll call round to-morrow.'

"'Do,' she sez. 'Me dog hasn't had a square meal for a week.'

"Chooper was highly delighted when he came back to the boat again.

"'The only way to treat girls,' he sez, 'is to take things for granted.'

"The funny thing about the whole business was that he'd fallen in love with this girl, and, by all accounts, he met her the next day and the next. The first day he called at her house, and she dropped a bucket of water on his head. The next day he met her in the village, and she threatened to give him in charge. The next day he wrote to her, and got his letter back with all the spellin' mistakes underlined in red ink.

"'That girl's gettin' quite fond of me,' sez the sanguine feller.

"'You'll never know how fond she is,' I sez, 'till she gets the strangle-hold on you and rubs your face with a brick.'

"But somehow or another Chooper had got it well fixed into his head that this Miss Pink (that was her name) was most desp'ritly in love with him.

"One night he came into barracks very wet, havin', he said, been caught in a shower.

"'Come over to Frimley with me,' he sez next day. 'I'm goin' to call on me young lady.'

"'Do you want somebody to protect you?' I sez.

"'No,' he sez, very off-handed—'no; we've made up our little misunderstandin's an' we're as thick as anythin'.'

"So to Frimley I went, though I didn't believe a word he said.

"By luck we met Miss Pink just outside the village, and when she see us she stopped dead in her stride.

"'What!' she sez. 'You again, you little rat!'

"Chooper smiled.

"'She always goes on like that,' he sez to me. 'It's only her fun.'

"'Fun!' she sez, flarin' up. 'What did I do to you last night?'

"'You chucked me into the canal,' sez Chooper, very calm; 'but I got out again.'

"'I pulled you out,' she sez.

"'Let bygones be bygones,' he sez, pleadin'. 'Where shall we go to-night—Gertrude?'

"'How dare you!' she sez, very wild.

"And with that she gave him a smack on the head that knocked him sideways.

"'Love,' he sez, in a mazy way—'it's love that makes you do that!'

"This went on for a long time. I found out in the meantime that this Miss Pink was a hockey champion, a long-walk champion, a dumb-bell champion, and a few other things; so I gathered from the fact that Chooper continued courting her, and remained alive to tell the tale, that she needed him to practise on. I found out, too, that she'd a tidy bit of money of her own.

"One Sunday afternoon this sanguine feller asked me to go walkin'.

"'Not me,' I sez—'if it's courtin' you mean. She'll start on me next.'

"But he persuaded me and I went.

"This Miss Pink, Chooper told me, lived in a nice little house with a maiden aunt.

"'I haven't met aunt yet,' sez Chooper. 'I call her "aunt" because she's as good as mine; but in a way I'm sorry for her—Gertrude wants some living with.'

"There was no sign of Miss Pink in the village, but after Chooper had walked up and down outside her house whistlin' very loud for about five minutes, half a brick came over the wall, followed by a cabbage.

"'That's her,' sez Chooper, with a sad smile; 'it's a sort of code—a brick means "Wait round the corner," a cabbage means—'

"Just then a potato came over the wall—whoosh! It caught Chooper in the neck.

"'What's that mean?' I sez; but he hadn't time to invent anythin' before the big, high garden gate was flung open, and out ran Miss Pink, looking very wrathy.

"'Mr. Chooper!' she sez.

"'She knows me name!' sez Chooper, ecstatic.

"'Mr. Chooper, or Choppers, or whatever your funny name is,' she sez, most exasperated, 'are you goin' to leave me in peace?'

"'I'll recite her a bit of poetry I made up,' sez Chooper, and pulls a paper out of his pocket.

I cannot eat, I cannot think,
I love a lovely girl named Pink.

"'That's you,' sez Chooper.

'She is the apple of my heart,
From her I'll never, never...'

"The girl leant against the wall an' looked at him.

"'I suppose I'll have to marry him,' she sez, talkin' to herself. 'He's a queer-lookin' little fellow, but he might be handy about the house.'

"In the course of time," said Smithy, "she married him. I didn't go to the weddin'—it wasn't safe—but I saw Chooper a few weeks afterwards.

"'You're a wonderful feller,' I said to him. 'Fancy perseverin' as you did with that girl! I suppose sanguineness is a gift?'

"He carefully stuck down the bit of sticking-plaster that was on his nose, and put another pin in the bandage that was on his wrist.

"'I ain't so sure it's a gift,' he sez, very slow and thoughtful. 'There's times when I think it's a bit of a vice.'"

CHAPTER IX

A DAY WITH THE CROWN PRINCE

"People," said Smithy, "talk about the hardships of soldierin', an' you'll find lots of misguided ole ladies sendin' Gen'ral French kneecaps an' wool mittens under the impression that he's havin' a bad time. There's some that pity the blokes in the trenches an' others that worry about the poor airmen, but the chap who sees what I might term the horrors of war is the O.C. Victories of the German Army.

"It's one of the hardest jobs in the world to get into the German Press Bureau. It requires a special trainin'. The officers are specially selected, an' have to pass an examination in military subjec's, as the Lie of the Land (Reconnaissance Department) an' Inventions (Engineerin' Department). Every feller has to serve three months in an English house-agent's office describin' Highly Desirable Properties situated in the heart of a Hunting Country (3 packs). Company's water, and Old-World Gardens, an' three months in an Income Tax Recovery Bureau. They then get on to the advanced course, where lyin' is done more scientifically—that is called the Diplomatic Service—an' they finish up with three months' prospectus writin'.

"They're then drafted to the German Press Bureau, with the rank of third-grade liar, an' gradually work up till they're in the same class as Miss Anna von Nias, that celebrated German lady.

"The work in war-time is very heavy. At 5 o'clock the reveille sounds, an' the first relief, springing out of bed, draw on their ink-proof pants, an' goose-step to the head factory.

"'Now, me lads,' sez the Colonel, 'to-day is the Kaiser's Birthday, an' I expect you to surpass yourselves. Let's have our usual Monday conference.'

"The German lie conference is more serious.

"'There's been some fightin' at Ypres,' sez the head Bureau chap. 'We took three prisoners.'

"'What regiments do they belong to?' sez another.

"'The Wigshires, the Killarnies, and the 1st Tipperaries,' sez the head chap.

"'Let's say we've took three regiments prisoners,' suggests another feller. By the time the conference is through them three fellers have grown into a division with artillery.

"'What about us?' sez the second in command.

"'We'd better say that we have taken Calais, but had to leave it owin' to the absence of decent hotel accommodation,' sez the chief.

"'Anything about Russia?' sez the second.

"'We took ten lines of Russian trenches,' sez the chief, writin' rapidly, 'an' we're only waitin' for the enemy to dig another an' we'll take that—how many prisoners did we take?'

"'We took 108 in the first attack an' 131 in the next,' sez the second, 'an' they took 10,000 of ourn.'

"'We took 108,131,' writes the chief, 'an' we lost 5—now what about the sea?'

"'We had a bad biffing on Sunday,' sez the second, 'an' lost a battle-cruiser an' a light cruiser; we shall have to own up to one of 'em.'

"'What does the British Official account say?' sez another factory worker.

"'It sez that the Admiral lost no opportunity and no time in comin' up to the raiders.'

"'Good,' sez the O.C. Victories, an' writes:—

'The British suffered a severe reverse. They admit the loss of H.M.S. No-Time and H.M.S. No-Opportunity, two of their grandest Dreadnoughts, and the proof of their sinking is contained in the official message that both ships 'came up'—probably before sinkin' for the last time. This is the truth.'

"It's a grand life," concluded Smithy; "in fact, I don't know anything finer. There's nothin' unpleasant to do, no hardship, no trouble—if you want a victory you pull out the drawer marked 'V' an' it's there.

"It's specially good when you can't get it in any other way.

"There's many things I'm glad I ain't," said Private Smith. "For instance, I shouldn't like to be a Belgian gun dog, and I shouldn't like to be the feller who has to explain away German victories; but, most of all, I shouldn't like to be the Crown Prince of Germany.

"We fellers that have stuck it in the trenches think we work an' suffer, but that young feller makes anythin' we do look like fish an' chips.

"'What's the day's programme, Hugo?' sez the Crown Prince, jumpin' out of bed in his bombproof pyjamas.

"'Exalted highness,' sez his valet, 'you're leadin' the Dead Head Hussars against the hated English.'

"'So I am,' sez the Prince, drinkin' a gallon of lager out o' a priceless Sevres vase wot he picked up on the battlefield; 'bring me armoured train to the door; tell the Princess I shall be late for dinner; an' send the proof of me new book, "Hints to Collectors; or, Hooks an' Crooks," to the publisher; unchain me favourite Zeppelin; an' bring me another jar of beer—war is hell,' he sez.

"Up comes Mrs. Crown Prince with the children.

"'Kiss your father,' she sez; 'he's got a rotten job.'

"In a few seconds the Crown Prince, entirely surrounded by Zeppelins, Prussian Guards, an' Dead Head Hussars, are dashin' madly to the frontier, singin' 'Dutch lads after Ale.'

"When he's not singin' that he's changin' his clothes, an' when he ain't changin' his clothes he's doin' strategy with the chief of the staff.

"'My idea,' sez the Crown Prince, 'is to move on the enemy's left an' by a lightnin' dash across the front to seize his right, or vice versa. You,' he sez to his general, 'you go in front an' draw the fire an' I'll lead a charge o' the Dead Heads—at least,' he sez, 'I would lead 'em, only it don't seem fair to take the job out of better an' more worthy hands,' he sez. 'Anyway, I'll be waitin' for you when you come back.'

"An' the charge is made, an' as many of the Dead Heads as can be spared come back, an' the Crown Prince makes a speech, jumps on to his armoured train, an' dashes madly back to Potsdam.

"That night a mysterious stranger, wearin' a black velvet mask, is admitted to the hospital in Brussels.

"Is it the Crown Prince? Who can say?

"The next mornin' he starts off for Russia wearin' a fur-lined overcoat, a skunk muff an' a top-knot of caviare.

"His father says good-bye to him on the station.

"'Farewell, Willie,' he sez. 'Conquer or die,' he sez.

"'Come back on your shield,' he sez. 'There ought to be a lot of shield in these Polish castles—gold ones.'

"'Farewell,' sez the Crown Prince, drawin' his sword. 'Never will I return,' he sez, 'till me proud feet are wearin' a hole in the neck of the haughty Muscovite.'

"'Don't forget what I said about dyin',' sez the Kaiser.

"'Trust me, mein farder,' sez Willie in fluent German.

"So everybody sings 'Dutch lads after Ale,' and, surrounded by Zeppelins, Prussian Guard, an' Newspaper Cuttin's, the intrepid youth flies to the infernal snows of Upper Poland.

"The joyous news is flashed forth. It reaches the Army.

"'Rejoice! The Crown Prince is hastenin' to join you.'

"The gen'ral staff turns pale. Von Hinkybug is observed to stagger.

"'Can't nothin' be done?' falters a fat general. 'Think of somethin', von Hinkybug—you're in charge of the strategy department.'

"'We might blow up the line,' sez Hinkybug thoughtful, 'or we might switch him on to the Warsaw branch.'

"But it is too late.

"The Crown Prince arrives, an', wipin' his feet on the prostrate figures o' the gen'ral staff, he tips the guard two Iron Crosses an' dashes madly into the Strategy House.

"'Bring up the 9th, 11th, 13th, an' 15th Corps,' he sez rapidly, 'deploy the cavalry, throw forward the artillery, an' let the battle begin.'

"'What a strategistical genius,' sez von Hinkybug, in such a low voice that he could be heard in the next block.

"The battle begins. It is watched with bated breath by the intrepid correspondents at Petrograd. The proceedin's are veiled in mystery.

'I have just heard glorious news,' wires Drummond Fife, 'I heard it from a friend in Moscow. He got it out of the papers. Ninety-six trains are on the way to Poland. They are empty trains. Why are they going to Poland? I can scarcely contain myself for joy. I can hardly digest me food. Oh, if the people of Petrograd knew what I know! Oh, if they did! Oh, if they could only read the Russian papers. Ninety-six empty trains! What does that news signify? I will tell you. It signifies four German Army Corps surrounded on two sides, battlin' desperately to get theirselves surrounded on three more sides. More to-morrow; but let me say this: The Crown Prince is directin' operations and has already been wounded and killed. The fate of Europe is hangin' in the balance. Nitchevo.'

"All day long the battle goes forward an' backward. The lunch score is:

Germans: 40,000 prisoners, 230 guns.
Russians: 50,000 prisoners, 235 guns.
(Russia in play.)

"Surrounded as they are, the Germans move northward. Reinforcements are hurried from Berlin. Two train-loads of Iron Crosses are flung into the conflict. Hinkybug is made a Field-Marshal, the Crown Prince is made a full corporal, Cracow is in flames, an' Prezimizzle falls for the sixty-third time in history.

"In the evenin' the Crown Prince returns home wet an' weary, just as the family have finished supper.

"'Why, here's Will!' sez the Kaiser. 'Pull your wet boots off, lad, an' bring a chair up to the table—mother's put a bit of rabbit in the oven for you, an' you'll find a bottle of beer under the table. Well, what's the news?'

"'I got the enemy on the run,' sez the Crown Prince.

"'Did they catch you?' sez the Kaiser, anxious.

"Nobody can realise," said Smithy, "the strenuosity of the Crown Prince's life. Scarcely a day passes but some Army Corps put a card in the winder inscribed

C.P.

an' off he goes to deliver the goods.

"'He is the idol of Berlin. People weep to see him go out to war. When he comes back they weep worse than ever. There is scarcely a dry eye in Unter den Linden as he passes on a wet day.

"Men swear by him; generals swear at him. There's some talk of gettin' up a testimonial to him an' raisin' the money for a wreath.

"His famous smile can be seen on every battlefield. Sometimes it's on one side of his mouth an' sometimes on the other.

"The Bavarians love him; the Austrians adore him; even the Russians follow him wherever he goes, an' the faster he goes, the faster they follow.

"To sum up, the Crown Prince is doin' two men's work, an' doin' it worse than six ordinary men.

"We're lookin' forward to seein' him," said Smithy. "We should like to call at his castle an' have a look round. It must be an interestin' place—the Lost Property Office of Europe, I call it."

CHAPTER X

NOBBY AND THE LAMB

"I'd like to meet Zepp'lin," reflected Smithy; "he must be the life an' soul of the German Staff just now.

"'I'm feelin' very depressed to-night, Willie,' sez the Kaiser, 'can'tyou suggest anything in the way of cheerin' me up?'

"'Come over to my dug-out, Pa,' sez the Crown Pinch, 'an' I'll show you a few articles I collected in France.'

"'I want somethin'comic,' sez the Kaiser.

"'I've had a new photo of myself taken nursin' a Belgian baby,' sez the Crown Pinch.

"'That's an old idea,' sez the Kaiser. 'I'll tell you what we'll do—'phone up ole Zepp'lin an' ask him to come along an' tell us a comic story.'

"So up comes Zepp'lin, an' in a few minutes the whole German Gen'ral Staff is holdin' his sides whilst he tells the hum'rous tale about the Balloon that carried Bombs for Ballast.

"'That reminds me,' sez Admiral von Tirkfitz, 'about a great joke I had with Scarborough—'

"'Did I tell you,' sez another feller, 'how we treated the British wounded at Cologne? Your High Frightfulness ought to hear this story—it'll make you ill with laughter...'

"An' so the merry evenin' wears on, the Grand Duke of Wartbug givin' an amusin' anecdote of the grand bonfire he had in the East of France, an' how him an' another chap killed a ferocious baby in self-defence.

"All these yarns about Zepp'lins droppin' ballast an' only hitting back when they're attacked reminds me of an old story which you may have heard.

"When we was in South Africa, Lord Roberts gave an order that any regiment caught lootin' would be sent to the base, an' the soldier concerned would be hung. That was Bobs' little way. When he gave an order you remembered it every time you buttoned your collar.

"Nobody wanted to loot because the only lootable things we found was abandoned wagons an' empty farmhouses, an' even the most hardened looter thought twice before he picked up these little trifles an' sent 'em home.

"But later, when columns was wanderin' all over the country, an' when the supply wagons temp'rally failed to connect, the temptation to invite a stray fowl or two to dinner was more than most fellers could stand.

"'What I feel,' sez Nobby one day, comin' into camp with his tunic bulgin' with dead birds, 'is that it would be cruelty to dumb chickens to leave 'em on the veldt to starve.'

"'Many of 'em,' he sez, as he started pluckin' the feathers off, 'have lost all their relations; their parents have died of sorrer an' their children are bein' served as omelettes at the officers' mess.'

"On the march up from Bloemfontein we struck a very hungry patch. The bridges were down an' some of the wagons must have got stuck in the drifts, an' it was emergency rations an' biscuits for us—or nothin'.

"'Nobby,' sez Spud Murphy, who was company cook at the time, 'why don't you go wanderin' round an' see if you can find an orphan chicken who wants a good home?'

"'Talk sense,' sez Nobby, 'how can there be any chicken w'hen Strathcona's Horse has been reconnoitrin' the ground?'

"None the less, he went on a foragin' expedition. He wandered almost to the outposts, an' every sentry he met he put a few inquiries to.

"'Have you seen anything of our regimental chicken?' he sez, so that nobody should think he was lootin'. An' then he explained that the chicken was a pet, an' marched ahead of the regiment. Nobby made up quite a pretty little story about that bird. How she laid an egg a day especially for the Colonel, an' how the War Office was allowing her a medal for alarmin' the camp by crowin' when we was attacked.

"Nobby was explaining all this to a corporal of one of the advanced posts when he saw somethin' that made him gasp.

"'There she is!' he sez, an' ran to a little hollow.

"'That ain't a chicken,' sez the corporal, 'that's a lamb.'

"Nobby lifted up the little baa-baa an' put it under his arm.

"'When I said "chicken,"' he sez, 'I referred to our regimental lamb—his pet name bein' "hicken."'

"Nobby, overjoyed, carried the lamb back to a place where nobody could see him.

"'Lambie,' he sez, 'I hate doin' it, but "B" Company is hungry.'

"He'd just finished his work an' his bayonet was still in his hand, when he heard a jingle behind him.

"Lookin' out of the corner of his eye he saw to his sorrow Lord Roberts an' his gilded staff, an' even in that short look Nobby saw a very unpleasant expression on Bobs' face.

"But Nobby wasn't easily upset.

"He gave the dead lamb another jab with his bayonet.

"'Fly at me, will you?' he sez, very loud. 'Bite me after I've fed you on bird seed, will you? Take that, you f'rocious blighter!'

"Bobs didn't smile and he didn't frown: he just looked at Nobby.

"'We seem to have arrived in time to save your life, my man,' he sez, in that quiet voice of his."

CHAPTER XI

SMITHY AND THE MISSING ZEP'LINK

"These," said Private Smith, of the 1st Anchester Regt., "these are stirrin' times. Zep'lins goin' up in France an' lights goin' down in London, provide what Nobby Clark calls the infernal law of consternation.

"Day an' night them Zep'lin factories are workin'. Situated in the same street as the Iron Cross works—Germany's staple industry—this magnificent Zep'lin foundry is in full swing.

"Every hour a bran' new Zep'lin slides down the Zepple-shoot, an' is seized by painters an' marked in plain figures:—

THIS IS A ZEPLIN.
IT IS VERBOTEN TO SPIT ON IT.

"The output is ten thousan' a week. The sky is full of 'em, an' the shootin' stars on root to a place in the sun are obliged to go round the other way.

"They are comin' to London nex' week. That's why we've got a navy. Two millions of 'em will be circulatin' round London after ten lookin' for a pub that's still open. As soon as it is found a bomb will be dropped, all the lights will go out by magic, an' the landlord's licence will be seized. On the fallin' of the second bomb all German waiters will be interned in the basement of the Evenin' News; on the third bomb Mr. McKenna will deliver his famous lecture on the great war of 1911 an' why it didn't come off.

"Every precaution is bein' taken. Regent Street an' Piccadilly Circus are passin' the night heavily disguised as Brookwood Cemetery. Motor buses that used to kill people in broad daylight are now killin' 'em by night. Everythin' is bein' done to cheer up a people at war. Next to a heavy casualty list, a walk through London by night is more invigoratin' than Fox's Book of Martyrs.

"Taxi-cabs are burnin' cheerful blue lights in order to deceive the wanderin' airmen that they're chemists' shops.

"The most you're likely to see here in the way of trouble is one of Nobby Clark's Zep'links.

"When we was in the trenches on the Marne, an argument rose one mornin' as to which was the biggest airship in the world.

"Some said 'Zep'lins' an' some said 'Clement Bayrums'—or whatever you call 'em.

"'You're wrong,' sez Nobby; 'the biggest airship in the world is the Zep'link.'

"'You mean the Zep'lin,' sez Spud Murphy.

"'I mean the Zep'link,' sez Nobby, very firm, 'so called because it's a sort of link between a Zep'lin an' an aeroplane. It's a thousand feet long, made of aluminium, an' is blown up with a special kind of gas. It carries three howitzers, a Black Maria, an' a regiment of the Prussian Guard.'

"'Don't you try to come it over me,' sez Spud; 'there never was a bulloon that could carry all that weight.'

"Nobby shrugs his shoulders.

"'Wait an' see,' he sez very mysterious. 'If a Zep'link come along an' dropped half a ton of guncotton on your fat head, would you believe me then?'

"'Is it likely?' sez Spud.

"Nobody believed in that Zep'link—not even when Nobby told the troops that it could fly so high that it was out of sight most of the time.

"'That's why you don't see it,' sez Nobby; 'but all the time you're sittin' there eatin' bully beef an' concoctin' letters for your relations, the Zep'link is looking down on you.'

"The next day the troops got a bit more believin', an' by the end of three days, them that wasn't slaying the hateful Huns were crickin' their necks lookin' out for Zep'links.

"It was highly amusing to Nobby an' hardly a day passed but he didn't find some new point about the Zep'link that he hadn't thought of before.

"If I'd had, what I might term the inventive genius of Nobby Clark, I'd have been layin' concrete gun-beds all over Germany.

"'The Zep'link,' sez Nobby, 'is provided with magnifyin' glasses so that the chap in charge can read the names of the reg'ments he's attackin' on their cap badges. It's got a patent dart-throwin' machine that can wipe out a brigade at a time. It's got nine guns mounted on the top, an' carries fifty 200-lb. shells, and the whole contrivance goes by electricity.'

"'It oughtn't to be allowed,' sez Spud, very indignant, 'it's against the Hague what-d'ye-call-it.'

"'It's got one of them too,' sez Nobby. 'It's no good, Spud, you've got to stand it—anyway,' he sez, 'nobody is goin' to miss you when, so to speak, you're called hence by the Zep'link.'

"The Adjutant come to hear of it, an' had a talk with Nobby.

"'Clark,' he sez, 'you're spreadin' alarm an' despondency amongst His Majesty's forces. The next time I hear about that fool Zep'link of yours, I'm goin' to give you a day's field punishment.'

"After that Nobby said no more, an' naturally havin' no time to gas, he had more time to think, an' he spent most of his time inventin' new parts to the Zep'link that he used to whisper in me ear when he was bivouacked for the night.

"Then he began to get serious, an' by the time we was entrenched on the north of the Aisne he wore that worried look which is usually only found in the face of the British soldier when he steps up to draw 14s. 8d. at the pay-table an' receives 9s. 7d.

"'What's the matter with you, Nobby?' I sez. 'You've only sung Tipperary three times since this mornin'—are you losin' your dash?'

"He looks round, an' he looks up.

"'Smithy,' he sez, very earnest, 'it ain't the Black Maria, an' it ain't the Prussian Guard,' he looks up again, searchin' the sky; 'it's this dam' Zep'link. Do you think there's anything in this yarn?'

"In my opinion," concluded Private Smith sagely, "it's the Zep'link that's expected in London."

CHAPTER XII

ON THE GERMAN FLEET

"If I hadn't been a soldier in the British Army," said Smithy enthusiastically, "I'd like to be a sailor in the German Navy. Next to bein' an anarchist or the Sultan of Turkey, or bein' one of them bright an' happy fellers that walks about the grounds of Colney Hatch knightin' the keepers, bein' a German sailor is one of the finest professions in the world.

"'Beg pardon, sir,' sez A.B. Schmidt, 'I've just cut a baby's head off.'

"'For why?' sez his officer.

"'Not standin' up an' salutin' when the band played "Dutch lads after Ale,"' sez the A.B.

"'You are a hero-patriot splendid,' sez the officer. 'Which will you have—at once—an Iron Cross or a marble clock?'

"'Marble clock,' sez the A.B., 'or the money,' he sez.

"Look at the life they live! Dashin' madly down the Kiel Canal an' dashin' madly back again, rocked in the cradle of the lock or facin' the deadly bloaters of Yarmouth trawlers.

"When one of them poor fellers goes to sea, he never knows whether he'll be home to tea or whether the accursed war-party will keep him busy till supper-time. Often the ships go out of harbour and minutes pass before they return.

"The Mayor and Corporation of Williams Haven come down to see 'em off.

"'Farewell,' he sez, speakin' with emotion. 'Go forth an' conquer,' he sez, 'the deadly enemy is waitin' for you—the eyes of the Fatherland is on you—so is the eyes of the Uncleland. A strong fishin' fleet, many of 'em armed with dum-dum mackerel, is at our gates.'

"The diary of a naval officer swept up by a mine-sweeper tells the story:

'1 o'clock.—We have left our dear fatherland—shall I ever forget it! How me heart beats.... We are now in deep water, and the ship is rollin'—but we are on our way! Travel brings out what is best in a man. Especially ocean travel.

'4 o'clock.—I am wounded—terribly. I have been in my bunk for two hours. Is it a wound or have I been poisoned? I feel a curious sensation. Oh, these English, how I hate them!

'8 o'clock.—We are off one of their deadly fortresses. It is called Brighton. The whole front is full of forts. My captain points out Fort Metropole, Fort Royal York (where all the Big Guns go), Fort Royal, Fort Victoria. Men are pulling machine guns.... Hundreds of them, along the front. They are shaped like bath chairs, but (my captain tells me) they usually contain an explosive charge. We see through our glasses cavalry horses being exercised at Rottingdean. We hear that Wireless is there!! Will he ever win a race? Who knows?

'8.15.—We are shelling Brighton, and the super-Dreadnought Skylark is throwing bricks at us. At last this is war!

'8.50.—We have silenced Fort Royal York, where the English Cabinet Minister Preston lives.

'8.55.—News has come that the police have been sent for. We are leaving—what a day!

'9.0.—The greatest vessel of the English Fleet, The Brighton Queen, attacked us, but we escaped in the fog.'

"Sometimes it's one fortified place, an' sometimes it's another. Sometimes the German Fleet go scourin' the Kiel Canal looking for the English fleet, but the cowardly British are never there.

"An' every time the Admiral goes out to look for the English an' don't find 'em, he gets an Iron Cross. It's worth it.

"'Once more you've saved the Fleet,' telegraphs the Kaiser. 'How can me an' God thank you! Am sendin' you (pay on delivery) a packet of Iron Crosses. Please give them to any of my gallant sailors who can find the missin' words in the following poem written by me:

'The German Fleet the British knocks,
But when we meet he'll give us—'

"'At the end of four months' (writes the Naval Correspondent of the Berliner Catbag), 'our Gran' Fleet is intact. Nothin' has happened to it. Let this be a lesson to every brave German. Spend your holidays at home, like our Navy does, an' keep the money in the country.'

"There's one thing certain about the German Navy," concluded Smithy, "we shall never be able to give 'em as good a hidin' as they're givin' theirselves."

"Nothin' depresses the German Navy worse than sinkin' a battle-cruiser an' a couple of Dreadnoughts.

"It doesn't depress Berlin, because Berlin don't know nothin' about the nerve strain of huntin' the British from the sea.

"'What's this?' sez the Kaiser to Von Tirkfitz, the celebrated man with the celebrated whiskers; 'what's this strange-lookin' biscuit tin with the dents?'

"'That, your Serene Godliness,' sez von Tirkfitz, 'is your cruiser-magnificent, Dirtflinger.'

"'I thought you said it wasn't damaged?' sez the Kaiser.

"'Not seriously damaged,' sez the Admiral; 'we never reckon that a ship is seriously damaged so long as it floats.'

"'Praise be to Allah!' sez the Kaiser; 'an' what is that strange-lookin' article in dry dock?'

"'That, your Worshipful Highness,' sez the Admiral, 'is our ever-grand and beautiful Sedlitz, what sank the Lion, Tiger, Panther, Leopard, an' Pussy Cat.'

"'Bishmallah!' sez the Kaiser; 'gather together as many of the crew as you've left, an' I'll say a few tender words of greetin'. After that, I'd like to have a few words with the head of the Frightfulness Department.'

"The conference is held behind closed doors. Sentries are posted at all the entrances, an' refreshments are passed through the winder at intervals.

"At the end of that time the new order is posted. It sez:

'We warn all peaceful ships not to approach England durin' the next five years. We won't tell you what we're goin' to do, but it's goin' to be something awful!'

"'That ought to do it,' sez the Kaiser, 'but we'll make things sure,' an' he issues another:

'We warn the French Army not to support the British on or about February 10. We can't say what we're goin' to do, but you can reckon on somethin' very dirty.'

"'Somethin' ought to be done about Russia,' sez von Falkenbug; 'von Hinkybug is gettin' very wild with the way he hasn't been supported.'

"'I'll soon settle that,' sez the Kaiser, an' issues a real terror.

'This is to give notice to the Russian Army that any attempt to advance along the Vistula will be met by very serious measures. We're doin' a certain thing in Poland that will spread terror and consternation throughout the world. Anybody who don't believe this will feel sick when it happens. Don't act the goat: be warned in time. This is for your own good.—(Signed) Wilhelm II.

'P.S.—Don't say I didn't warn you.'

"'An',' sez the Kaiser, 'it that don't upset the Gran' Duke Nicholas, I'm a square-headed Dutchman.'

"An' now the whole world sits down to watch the new way of makin' war take shape. All the neutral countries an' Roumania, all the b'ligerent countries an' Italy, all the pro-German countries, if any, sit with bated breath.

"The British Fleet goes over an' under the North Sea, the Russian Army goes in an' out the German trenches, the French Army goes up an' down the Vosgis, an' every minute we are expectin' to hear the worst. Will it happen?

"Opinion is divided. Some say yes, an' some say no. What will it be? Some think it will be a submarine Zeppelin, others say it may be a Flyin' Dreadnought with green funnels. Will it explode? Who knows?

"Things don't go as fast as the Kaiser would like. He calls another meetin' of the Frightfulness Lodge. The minutes of the last meetin' are read an' confirmed. Brother Wilhelm, Chief Fright (in the chair), moves a vote of confidence in the Chairman. Carried. Brother Wilhelm, junior (Vice-Fright), moves an address of welcome to the Hero of Longwy. Carried. Brother Hinkybug (Worshipful Bogey) moves a vote of thanks to the Conqueror of Warsaw. Carried. The Hymn of Hate is now sung by the lodge upstanding.

"It is proposed an' seconded that Scarborough shall in future be marked 'Fort Scarborough' on all German maps. Carried.

"'Worthy brethren,' sez the Chief Fright, 'I propose that we issue a new proclamation: the Secretary will now read same.'

"Brother Bestman-Golliwog (Frightful Scribe and Keeper of the Golden Lyre) reads:

'The German nation gives notice that in future it will ignore the British Navy, an' will land 10,000,000 on the coast of Yorkshire. Any attempt on the part of the English railway companies to refuse to carry the army to London will be frightfully resented. Any attempt on the part of the British Navy to hamper our transports will be dealt with accordin' to law. This is our last warnin'. We don't want any more trouble; a nod's as good as a wink.—Wilhelm.'

"I hear from time to time," said Smithy, "that our Navy prevents Germans gettin' contraband. Copper's contraband because you make shells with it. Coal's contraband, an' lead's contraband. But I'm lookin' forward to the day when the Government makes ink contraband—that'll finish the war."

CHAPTER XIII

On W.O. Genius

"There's no doubt," said Smithy thoughtfully, "that somewhere in the War Office there is what I might term the grandest mind that was ever heard tell about. It ain't an ordinary mind—it's just one big idea, an' the main idea is to help recruitin'.

"I don't know who the feller is so I'll call him Henry. He may be a gen'ral, he may be a colonel, he may be anything in the world, but I'll stake me boots an' cholera belt on his not bein' a private.

"Henry thinks of nothin' else, mornin', noon and night, but ideas for raisin' recruits.

"Often and often he puts his shirt on inside out, goes down the office in his bedsocks, owin' to his mind bein' too full of recruitin' to trouble about dressin' hisself properly.

"One day he has one idea, another day he has two. Sometimes he wakes up in the middle of the night, an' jumpin' out of bed writes furiously till daybreak. At other times he sleeps.

"He comes down to the Grand Military Recruitin' Room one day lookin' radiant an' happy.

"'I got a grand idea as I was washin' my neck,' he sez; 'let's put all the lights out an' shut all the pubs.'

"So they done it, but recruits didn't come any faster, owin' to their bein' required at home to sweep up the bits of Zeppelins that was expected to fall in the garden. So he blamed McKenna.

"Another day he came down to the office dancin' with joy.

"'What's the height standard for the infantry?' he sez.

"'Five-foot-four,' sez one of the experts.

"'Let's make it five-foot-six,' he sez, 'to encourage the people to grow.' That didn't bring 'em in so he blamed McKenna again.

"Then he discovered that pals who enlisted was allowed to serve together in the same regiment.

"'Stop that,' he sez, 'it keeps fellers out of the Army who haven't got any friends.'

"Somehow that didn't increase the number of recruits.

"'McKenna again!' sez the public; 'dam' that feller, why doesn't he leave the Army alone?'

"But what put the flagstaff on all Henry's ideas was the one he picked up when he was dinin' with Lady X—.

"Henry called the War Office Staff together in the middle of the night.

"'I've got a new one,' he sez, tremblin' with pride; 'let's put the soldiers' wives under police supervision. It will give the men confidence,' he sez, 'to know that their wives are bein' looked after. It will make our gallant fellers in the trenches fight better, it will bring recruits by the million.'

"The War Office knows a lot," said Smithy; "it knows that sentiment is nothin'. Fellers stand up in the House of Commons an' say 'K.' ain't got any sentiment at all (laughter).

"Sentiment is a rum thing; scraps of paper are sentiment, patriotism is sentiment; the feelin' that makes one regiment hold a line of trenches an' another give way is sentiment; sentiment is holdin' on to Ypres until hell freezes.

"Men aren't fightin' for one-an'-two a day—they're not chuckin' their lives away for a five-bob medal— they aren't sufferin' for anything that you can put on a cheque.

"If you cut out sentiment from soldierin' you're cuttin' out somethin' that contractors can't supply an' Woolwich Arsenal can't make.

"They ought to get rid of Henry an' give his sleepin' accommodation to a feller who has a Union Jack over his bed an' can't go to sleep till he has heard 'Rule Britannia' on the gramophone.

"He ought to have the wall of his room covered with pictures, pictures of them sentimental soldiers goin' down on the Birkenhead, pictures of sentimental Highlanders throwin' back the Russian cavalry at Balaklava, pictures of sentimental Captain Oates goin' out to die in the blizzard.

"Any fool can laugh at sentiment—you find civilians who laugh at God.

"The general who doesn't know the value of sentiment has had his military education neglected.

"My own view of the situation," said Smithy, "can be put in a few words. A civilian named Tennant said that 'K.' hadn't any sentiment. That's not true. 'K.' is a sentimentalist, and Tennant is a liar.

"As for Henry, with his grand ideas for gettin' recruits, I'd settle him in two jiffs.

"I'd hang him—for the duration of the war only."

CHAPTER XIV

ON RECRUITING

"There was a feller of ours named Hokey, who had a brother—he's got him still, because Hokey's brother is one of those fellers who are pretty difficult to lose.

"When the war broke out young Hokey was a sailor on a P.O. boat, but naturally bein' a true-born Briton he told the head steward—that being the sailor department young Hokey was in—that as soon as he got to England he was goin' to enlist.

"'My country wants energetic an' fearless men,' sez young Hokey, 'an' I'll see that she gets me. Me for the cavalry—for if there's one thing I like more than another it's a good nag. I've got military blood in me veins, sir,' he says.

"'Go and put some naval blackin' on my boots,' sez the chief steward.

"When young Hokey got to England, he made up his mind to have a few days' rest, an' went to stay with a married sister—his sister, not anybody else's sister—down Deptford way.

"'I'm goin' to war,' he sez, 'it's me duty an', so to speak, me pleasure.'

"'Good for you, Horace,' sez his sister, an' when some of the neighbours came in to get Horace's opinion on the war, she told 'em.

"'He's going to enlist,' she sez, 'an' he's come all the way from abroad to do it.'

"'It's me military spirit,' sez young Hokey modestly.

"The mornin' after he'd arrived in England he went up to Town, an' the first thing he saw was a big poster which said:

'RECRUITS WANTED AT ONCE.
FOR THE DURATION OF THE WAR ONLY.'

"'That's me,' sez young Hokey, very pleased.

"On the back of his tram ticket was the words 'England needs you,' and young Hokey smiled. 'That's me too,' he sez.

"At Charin' Cross was a great big poster that said '100,000 men wanted at once—don't shirk.'

"'Who's shirkin'?' sez young Hokey, indignant.

"All that day wherever he went he was met by big pictures an' big placards callin' on him to 'Be a Man.' He saw it in the tube lift, an' he saw it on the newspaper placards. He couldn't turn his head without meetin' a picture of Lord Kitchener with the words, 'It's YOU I want!'

"When he got down into the bowels of the earth an' took his seat in a tube train there was another notice starin' him in the face.

'WILLIN' MEN ARE HAPPY FIGHTERS.
DON'T WAIT TILL THE TRENCHES ARE DRY,
ENLIST NOW AND GET PATRIOTIC CHILBLAINS.'

"'Oh, hell!' sez young Hokey, an' went home out of spirits.

"The next day he nipped down to Brighton. Walkin' along the front he met a beau-chus young girl who was wearin' a hundred pounds' worth of furs round her neck, an' was knitting a fourpenny ha'penny pair of mitts for the heroes of old England.

"'Excuse me,' she sez, lookin' him straight in the eye, 'England wants you.'

"'I dare say,' sez young Hokey.

"'Don't shirk,' sez the young lady.

"Young Hokey glares at her an' goes on.

"He came back to London, and went into a music-hall. The first turn was a lady who knelt on the stage an' stretched out her arms to young Hokey.

"'I don't want to lose you,' she sings, 'an' I think you ought to go, your King an' your country—bo-oth need you so....'

"Young Hokey went out an' tried another music-hall. He was happy whilst a chap was jugglin' cannon balls, but the next turn was a lady in short frocks who sang—

'I don't want to lose you
But I think...'

"Young Hokey went home.

"On his way to Deptford a fat old chap sittin' opposite in the railway carriage leans over an' sez:

"'Excuse me, sir—don't you think you ought to be with your friends in the trenches?'

"'I ain't got any friends in the trenches,' growls young Hokey.

"'We want every man in this war,' sez the old gent.

"'I ain't every man,' sez young Hokey.

"'Don't you love your country?' sez the old chap sternly.

"'No,' sez Hokey.

"'He's a German!' sez the old chap; 'I suspected it all along.'

"'That puts the lid on it,' sez young Hokey, an' the next mornin' before anybody was up he packs his traps an' goes down to the docks.

"'Hullo,' sez the chief steward, 'what do you want?'

"'I want to sign on for the next voyage,' sez young Hokey.

"'But I thought you was goin' to enlist?' sez the chief steward.

"'So I was,' sez young Hokey.

"'I thought you was going into the cavalry,' sez the chief steward. 'You told me you was lookin' forward to a nag.'

"'I was, sir,' sez young Hokey, 'but not the kind of nag I've been having lately.'"

CHAPTER XV

THE STRATEGIST

"We are confronted with a serious situation," Private Smith hastened to inform me when I entered the ward which has the honour of housing him till his toe heals. "The great heart of England is throbbing like mad, and there is doubt in every mind, suspicion in every brain.

"Are we doing as well as can be expected? Is the Navy still knocking about? What's wrong with our strategy?

"England is goin' to be invaded. 'It's a perfec'ly absurd idea,' writes The Times military correspondent, 'but what am I to do? My plan for the German is this: come out an' fight the British Navy, an' whilst everybody's lookin' that way, send a quarter of million Germans across the sea an' land 'em somewhere. The best way of gettin' 'em to England is by ships. The duty of Englishmen is clear. Seize the nearest uniform an' get into it. Policemen's uniforms are easiest to seize. Havin' done this, all is plain sailin', for, as dear old Claude Snitch sez, do your best, if you can't do anything better.

"'In the meantime, the initiative is passin' from the War Office. The campaign is now in the hands of Winston Churchill an' the Morning Post. Why did Antwerp fall? Some people think it was because of the Germans, but the whole hijeous situation is now revealed. It was Winston. By sendin' ten thousand sailors to Antwerp he let it fall. Will France fall? It is a serious thought. It is an open secret that there is a British army there. Let us find out the feller that sent it an' replace him. If there is another reason for Antwerp fallin', it is because there was a Belgian army there too. Who was responsible for this? We seriously warn our readers that the conduct of the war is now in the hands of amateurs—there isn't a single newspaper expert on the War Office staff!'

"By the time I read the newspapers through," said Smithy, "an' have found the little paragraphs that all the big headlines are about, by the time I've read what the wounded soldier told the policeman an' what the policeman said to the reporter, I begin to rattle meself to death.

"We've got a strategist in our regiment called Gooley. Henry Arthur Hector Goole his proper name, an' if he hadn't been born in what I might term humble or Deptford circumstances, he'd have made a good general—cook-general.

"After the battle of Mons, when we was edgin' away from Mauberje, Gooley, me an' Nobby was in the same set of fours.

"'What I should have done if I'd been French,' says Gooley, 'is to strike straight into Germany, cut the communication cords, get round the rear of the enemy, an' then where would the Kaiser be?'

"'Ah!' sez Nobby, 'that's the question.'

"'What I should have done,' sez Gooley, 'would have been to send the Anchesters to make a flank attack on the left. I should then have sent the Belgian...' an' so on.

"'Where would the Kaiser be then?' sez Gooley again.

"So Nobby told him.

"'Never havin' a vulgar mind,' sez Gooley, 'I won't foller your argument. Take this place, for instance—' 'an' he waved his hand round the country.

"It was pretty to watch—especially the Wigshires bein' shelled as they moved along the slope of a hill. Never seen the 1st Wigshires movin' quick, have you? Well, if you'd seen 'em that day you'd have thought they was riflemen.

"'My idea,' sez Gooley, 'is this: we oughtn't to be retirin' at all. What we ought to do is to take up a position on that hill where the wood is, dig ourselves in, an' turn old von Gluck's left—'

"He'd hardly got the words out o' his mouth when the Adjutant came gallopin' along the line.

"He stopped by the Colonel, an' we, bein' in the leadin' fours, heard him.

"'Will you take your men to that hill on the right and cover the retirement of the 1st Division?' he sez.

"A minute later we had left the road an' was movin' on the hill. We got there at two o'clock, and at 2.1 the German guns got to hear about it. From 2 to 5 they shelled us, droppin' about 350 a minute.

"There we lay, crouched up close to the ground, firin' as an' when we could, but spendin' most of the time wonderin' if the family would go into mournin'.

"In the height o' the firing, Nobby crawled up to Gooley's side an' landed him a horrid kick.

"'Hullo, strategist,' hissed Nobby, 'how do you like it?'

"Poor old Gooley looked round, an' for a bit hadn't a word to say.

"'It's my mistake,' he sez; 'this ain't strategy, it's tactics.'

"And," concluded Smithy, "there's lots of newspaper fellers that's making the same mistake. Strategy is good, an' tactics is good, but using military strategy for party tactics is rotten."

"Bein' a strategist ain't like bein' a poet—you have to be born to be a poet, you've got to be dead before you're a good strategist.

"Mokey was a good strategist, so was Napoleon, so was Wellin'ton—they're all passed to what Nobby calls the Great Behind. The Kaiser's a rotten strategist—he's alive. I'm hopin' the Crown Prince'll be a great strategist too, soon, but all the reports from the seat of war show that he's in good health.

"There are ten ways of winnin' battles. Nine of 'em is to have half as many troops again as the enemy, an' the other way is to have twice as many.

"Nowadays strategy don't count for much. Suppose the Kaiser was attackin' the British.

"'How many men have we got?' he sez.

"'Almighty Goodness,' sez his head general, 'we've got about half a million more than the enemy.'

"'Then I'll have to try some of my strategy,' sez the Kaiser.

"'Hold hard, your Imperial Hunship,' sez the head general. 'I'll wire for reinforcements.'

"If you was to have a competition in the German Army to find out what was the most popular thing in the world the figgers would be:

Sudden Death... 9,753
Typhoid Fever... 6,347
The British Navy... 2
The Kaiser's Strategy... 1

"That's, of course, if the Kaiser had a vote.

"I'm not sayin' that there's no strategy in Germany. There must be a lot. They got it through neutral countries, an' it was labelled 'cotton.' The only kind of strategy that's worth anything is bought by the ton in America an' shipped through Holland.

"There's another kind, as any one who reads the latest reports from the front knows.

"A council of war is called, an' the Kaiser comes, lookin' pale an' haggard, wearing a mystic infectuous smile. His hair is white, an' he arrives chantin' a battle hymn.

"The Crown Prince comes in, his pockets bulgin' with strategy that he's picked up in the French chat-oos.

"The Kaiser takes his seat.

"'Where's the Sluis correspondent of the Tyd?' he sez.

"'Under the table, your Supreme Royalty,' sez General von Kluck.

"'Let the proceeding start,' sez the Kaiser. 'I have called you here to get your advice on the strategy of the war. I think we ought to crush the English an' annihilate the Russian. We will attack Warsaw an' Ypres, an' after that cross the English Channel an' sack London. I shall be glad to know what you think of my idea. Don't let anybody speak or there'll be trouble. I am German Mike, an' me word is law.— Anybody any questions to ask?—Carried unanimously. The meetin' is adjourned, an' me son Willie will now entertain you with a selection on his loot. Boy, bring me a Villa-Villa.'

"Sometimes the Kaiser gets a bigger idea than at other times. Take Scarborough, for instance.

"'There's a fortified fortress with forts called Scarborough,' he sez; 'it's heavily entrenched, an' is believed to be the headquarters of them ferocious boy scouts I've heard about.'

"'Go forth, Henry, mein brutter, an' reduce it to rags,' he sez, 'like mv nerves,' he sez.

"'Is that good strategy, Holy Relation?' sez Henry.

"'It's safe,' sez the Kaiser.

"'But,' sez Henry, 'suppose one of them Dreadnoughts come up an' biff me?'

"'They wouldn't do anything so inhuman,' sez the Kaiser, 'but if they did I'd report the matter to me friend President Wilson, because,' he sez, 'if you an' your gallant comrades was sunk, America would lose good customers, an' if they lost good customers there would be a trade depression in America an' me friend Wilson would send one of his famous notes.'

"Strategy," Smithy went on, "is the art of deceivin' your enemy into believin' that he's deceivin' you. German strategy is the art of deceivin' yourself,

"The progress of Gen'ral von Hinkybug showed you what good strategy is. Hinkybug is a grand strategist. One of the first things he did when he was made a gen'ral was to get a telephone wire laid on to the Kaiser.

"'Give me Almighty No. 1 Potsdam,' sez Hinkybug. 'Is that your Serene Holiness? It is? I'm salutin' you— you can't see it, but it's true. The photographic correspondent of the Damberg Tagblud is takin' me picture. I just wanted to say that I am victorious all along the line. I thought you'd like to know—yes, all along the line. I could get a third-class ticket to Warsaw for a pfennig, only the trains ain't runnin'. Good morgans, komrade! Hoch!'

"The next day he rings him up again.

"'Is that you, Angel Face? It is; I beg to report that I am victorious all along the line. I've took Oomstockovo, Doomstockovo, and Pzmerz.'

"'Good for you, Hinky,' sez the Kaiser; 'cut yourself an Iron Cross.'

"'I've got one, your Magnificent Splendour,' sez von Hinkybug. 'Could I have a set of trousers stretchers?'

"'Yes,' sez the Kaiser, 'gold ones. Hoch!'

"'Hoch!' sez Hinkybug.

"Two days later von Hinkybug gets on to Almighty No. 1 and the Kaiser's voice answers him.

"'I'm victorious all along the line, your War Lordship,' he sez, 'everybody is in retreat—includin' the Austrians,' he sez.

"'Fine,' sez the Kaiser; 'what a strategist is lost in you, Hinkybug!'

"When he rings off the Kaiser calls up the exchange.

"'If that feller Hinkybug calls me up to-morrer,' he sez, 'tell him I'm spending New Year's Day in a Zeppelin,' an' to make sure he sends out a troop of Uhlans to cut all the telephone wires.'

"This war will be won by strategy," concluded Smithy, "the strategy of the Gen'ral Staff hidin' the fac's from Berlin an' the strategy of Berlin hangin' the Gen'ral Staff; but what's goin' to finish the business quicker than anything else is sendin' 500,000 of Kitchener's strategists to France in the spring armed with strategic rifles an' bayonets, an' strategi-in' theirselves all over the Kaiser's army."

CHAPTER XVI

SMITHY SURVEYS THE LAND

Removed, as he is, for the moment from the immensely fascinating business of war, Private Smithy, who is, before all other things, a philosopher, devotes his attention nowadays to study of mankind in its relations to patriotism.

"Never," said Smithy, nursing his wounded foot and speaking with that heavy enthusiasm which veils so many sentiments, "never in me life have I seen such patriotism as there is over this war.

"In Parliament Patriot Asquith shakes han's with Patriot Balfour, an' Patriot Bonar Law shakes han's with Patriot Lloyd George—who ain't been called a thief for so long that he'll forget what it feels like. An' Patriot Christabel Pankhurst shakes han's with the stomach-pump an' ties a Union Jack round the forcible feeder.

"Everywhere everybody's doin' their best for the dear ole Empire on the understandin' that the dear ole Empire will do its whack when the time comes round.

'I'm sixty-two,' writes one patriot to his favourite tuppenny paper, 'an' I'm as young now as ever I'm likely to be,' he sez. 'Can't some use be made of me? I can run, jump, swim, weed gardens, play hop-scotch, an' the organ. I have offered myself as a general, and yet,' he sez, 'nobody leaps at me: an' they talk about the shortage of officers!'

"Patriot young ladies are sellin' patriotic flags for patriotic objects. Patriot cabmen are defendin' the empire by flyin' the flags of all nations an' askin' their fares to join the army.

'I have given up eatin' German sausage,' writes Trueheart of Putney. 'Can't somethin' be done to stop German yeast risin' in our very midst?'

"All over the shop the same feelin' prevails: people are urgin' each other to enlist; young ladies who usually spend their lives stickin' feathers in their hats are now stickin' feathers in other people's coats. An' our wounded soldiers (God bless 'em!) we can't do enough for 'em! We're givin' 'em dressing jackets, hair-combs, hatpins, trousers stretchers, an' other medical comforts.

"Day by day the columns of the Press are filled with the narratives of our heroic defenders. "Private Spud Murphy writes:

'It was like hell in the trenches, an' when the shrapnel burst it was like hell, an' when it didn't burst it was like hell. Everything was hell, includin' the bully-beef.'

"Corporal juggy Jones writes:

'Nothing has reminded me so much of hell as that day before Paris.'

"All the space that ain't devoted to hell is taken up with the predictions of the military experts.

'The Germans,' writes Captain X, the military critic of the Drapers' Herald, 'now occupy the line Hier-Thair. Will they be pushed off? It is a great day for England. My idea is that if a million Russians could be landed on the line Hyer-Huppe or the line Loer-Doun, or the railway line, or even on a clothesline, the enemy would be awfully surprised. O if the country had only listened to my warnin' in 1904! O if they'd only read my book, England and the War after Next (a few copies of which may still be obtained by mentionin' my name and six shillin's in the same breath), we should have had a great army now! Thanks to my book, Dreadnaughts or Draughts, we have got a navy.'

"I am amazed," said Smithy soberly, "at the sacrifices the civilian population are makin'. They have even sacrificed all chance o' the soldier gettin' drunk after eleven.

"Everybody is doin' somethin' for the cause. Theatrical managers are keepin' their theatres open to employ the poor actors; the actors are workin' on half salaries for the benefit of the poor managers, lots o' businesses that have made a steady loss for the last ten years are givin' half their profits to the Prince's fund. An' the women!—ah, the women are splendid!

"Girls are neglecting the house work to volunteer as Red Cross nurses: they have felt the call of England, and obeyed. They've got the uniform an' a pair of scissors, an' now all they want is a few patients to practise on. England, my England!

"The song writers are workin' overtime. There's one young feller that's sounded the clarion note—it strikes a thrill through every heart.

'What will I say, sonny; what will I say
When they ask "Did you carry a gun?
Did you march with the band to the arrogant land
And harass the horrible Hun?"
What can I say, sonny; what can I say?
I shall answer with pride, my dear chap,
I'm a poet all right, but poets don't fight—
They urge on the others to scrap.

"Every day The Times is filled with poetry. You know that it's poetry because the lines all begin with capital letters. It's poetry, though. It makes you choke—an' spit. Never in the history of the world was there such poetry; it may be many years before there is anything like it—with luck.

"An' we're goin' to capture German trade. Everybody's excited about it. There was a feller in here the other day—the sister will remember his name; he had whiskers—who could talk of nothin' else.

"'We're goin' to get the whole of the German commerce,' he sez, very enthusiastic. 'Take textiles,' he sez.

"'I'm takin' magnesia,' I sez.

"'I mean take textiles,' he sez, rapid. 'We imported or exported (I forget which) ninety millions—think o' that! What we've got to do,' he sez, 'is to smash the German Fleet, hang the Kaiser, get the trade, an' leave everything else to luck.'

"England," Smithy went on impressively, "never stood so firm. She's on the Right Side; the authors, after due consideration an' much heart-searchin', have written to say so. Them that haven't written wasn't asked. When the troops see that letter they'll go mad with joy. When the Wigshires, an' Anchesters, an' the Bloodshires learn that Mr. Jarvis, tire celebrated author of Her Soulmate; or, Parted by a Cruel Stepmother, has given his consent to the war, they won't be able to fight for laughin'. Everybody who is anybody has done somethin' for England. There ain't a patriot from Highgate to Norwood who hasn't sent at least two letters to the paper.

"Robert Scratchford, the celebrated Socialist, is writin' a page every week. What does he say?

'The British boys are wonderful, they are unique, they are brilliant. They are in France, fighting; they are marchin', they are singin', perhaps they are dancin'. I went down to Aldershot last week. I was goin' by the 10.40, but I missed the train; I caught the 1.15. It was a nice railway carriage. I came back by the 5.40 and a soldier got in. He said that he'd been turned out of another railway carriage because they wouldn't let him smoke. The cowards! They wouldn't let him smoke in a non-smoker. "It was like hell—

Mons," said the soldier, with a far-away look, in which horror, rage, hope, hunger, benevolence, an' pain struggled for supremacy, "an' they wouldn't let me smoke in a non-smoker... after Mons!"

'No, reader, I am not inventin' this story,' continues the intrepid writer. 'Every bit is true, includin' the dots between the words.'

Smithy lit a deplorable cigarette with tender care and breathed smoke through his nostrils.

"Out there"—he jerked his head France-ward, "we've got our troubles the same as Germany. There's a Kaiser in every regiment, I should say; anyway, there was one in the Anchesters. Slob his name is—Slob Jones, of B Company. That feller is (or was) one of the most celebrated speech-makers in the army.

"At cricket dinners, A.T.A.* meetin's, Christmas Days, an' canteen soirees Slob would up an' speak his mind.

* Army Temperance Association.

"He used to make speeches to recruits about their country, an' they used to make speeches to him about his face. He'd address meetin's in the back-field, on the ranges, on the line o' march, an' it was always about the dear ole land.

"Suppose a fatigue party was told off to weed the colonel's garden.

"'Go forth,' sez Slob, 'go forth an' fructify the earth; let one blade of grass show where two grew before. Show no mercy to the slugs; make your name as terrible to the worms as the name of Arthur Zerksees was to Arry Stottles.'

"A rare feller he was for diggin' up old-fashioned names, an' the way he used to talk about Juleus Cæsar ought to have made that celebrated officer turn in the grave.

"When we got to France, Slob was in his element. He used to address all the villages we stopped at.

"'Friends,' he sez, 'I bring you good tidin's,' he sez. 'The day has dawned an' the night has passed, an' the afternoon is comin', and so is tomorrow mornin'. Devote your attention to General French's contemptible little army, beginnin' on me,' he sez. 'I'm open to any attention that looks or smells like food,' he sez.

"Poor ole Slob!" reflected Smithy, shaking his head sadly. "He went out one afternoon on outpost duty and met a party of Uhlans. A chap of the 19th Hussars brought the news.

"'One of your chaps has been pinched,' he sez.

"'Who by?' sez Nobby Clark.

"'By the Uhlans,' sez the Hussar chap. 'I was lyin' doggo behind a hedge an' I see 'em go by. He was talkin' to them Uhlans somethin' awful about culture an' the sacred rights of man, an' they was listenin', sort of awe-struck.'

"'That's bad,' sez Nobby, 'for Germany,' he sez. 'The Kaiser's bad enough an' Slob's bad enough, but with the Kaiser an' Slob in the same country Germany will be a rotten hole—it will be like hell,' he sez."

CHAPTER XVII

LIEUTENANT X

"All the news from the front is favourable," said Private Smith, after a pause; "but I'm not so sure that it wouldn't be more favourable if the despatches was in the hands of a chap o' 'B' Company named Morses.

"Herbert Morses his name is, or was, an' next to Nobby Clark one of the finest despatch writers that ever drew the breath of life.

"Nobody ever knew what Morses did with his money; but that didn't worry 'em so much as tryin' to discover what he did with theirs.

"Morses was a great chap for borrowin' money. Sometimes he wanted it to send home to the old folks, sometimes he wanted to do a pal a turn, an' sometimes it was to save a soldier's widder from bein' turned out o' house and home by a cruel lan'lady.

"But one thing you could gamble on, he never wanted the money for himself, an' when chaps went to him for their bit o' stuff he was always mysterious an' dreamy.

"'I can't talk to you about it here,' he sez, 'not in public—I'll write to you.'

"'What's the good o' writin' to me when I'm sleepin' in the bed next to you?' sez the chap he owed it to, indignant. 'Four an' a tanner I let you have to save an ole pensioner from starvation.'

"'I'll write to you,' sez Morses; 'we'd better have it down in black an' white.'

"An' them letters o' his was wonderful. I lent him half-a-bar once, an' got literature to last me a month. It was all about the weather an' the state of England's Navy, an' the horrible economic condition of the East End, but nothin' about money.

"To read Morses' letter you'd have thought that there wasn't such things in the world as four half-crowns.

"Just about this time Nobby Clark was batman to a young officer of ours, whose name has been suppressed by the Press Bureau, an' whom I will call or term Lieutenant X.

"A nice young feller was Exy, full of life an' a desire for change—small change. Ten letters by every post, an' all that hadn't a ha'penny stamp on 'em was registered with the solicitor's name on the flap.

"One mornin', goin' through his correspondence, he sort of sat back an' groaned.

"'Clark,' he sez, 'I'm done for.'

"'Yes, sir,' sez Nobby, knowin' nothin' about it.

"'I'm done,' sez Lieutenant X., 'if I can't stave off this dam creditor I'm—my name is mud.'

"Nobby thought a bit.

"'Why not lure him down here an' get some of our chaps to set about him, sir?' sez Nobby; but Lieutenant X. shook his head.

"'It can't be done,' he sez, 'it's me uncle in the War Office.'

"It appears that Lieutenant X., in a lighthearted moment, had drawn a hundred from his rich uncle till Monday. He didn't say what Monday, but after about a hundred Mondays had come an' gone General G (that was his uncle) began to get worried an' sent Lieutenant X. a calendar with

'Sunday's child is full of grace,
Monday's child has lost his place,'

on it.

"And he follered this up with an insulting letter.

"'I've got to do somethin', Clark,' groans Lieutenant X. 'My uncle bein' at the War Office can hand me one.'

"'Write to him, sir,' sez Nobby.

"'What can I write?' sez Lieutenant X.

"'I'll think it out, sir,' sez Nobby.

"One day Nobby comes to me.

"'Smithy,' he sez, 'I've just lent Mossy two bob.'

"'Are you ill?' I sez.

"'Not critically,' sez Nobby, 'but the patriotic feller wants to subscribe to the Navy League an' I hadn't the heart to refuse him.'

"The very next day Nobby wrote to Mossy an' asked for his money back. It was a funny thing for him to do, for his way of collectin' debts is to get the feller alone an' chew his ear off.

"Morses wrote back thankin' Nobby for bein' such a gentleman as to write, an' tellin' him the latest news from Newmarket.

"Nobby wrote again next day, an' that same afternoon had eight pages about how the little birds fly home to their southern clime when the leaves begin to fall.

"He wrote reg'lar every day—sometimes it was all about drink an' the evils of bettin', an' sometimes it was about Home Rule—but it was never about the two bob he owed Nobby.

"An' every letter he wrote Nobby took to Lieutenant X., who done it up into proper English an' sent it off to his uncle at the War Office.

"One day Lieutenant X. was very happy.

"'Pack my kit, Clark,' he sez, 'I'm off to the War Office.'

"'Beg pardon, sir,' sez Nobby, 'I hope the General's acted fair to you.'

"'Yes, Clark,' sez Lieutenant X., 'he's forgiven the loan an' appointed me to the staff. He sez a man who can write pages about every subject under the sun except the subject he's supposed to be writin' about, is wasted in a regiment.'

"I often wonder," added Smithy thoughtfully, "if Lieutenant X. is at the front."

CHAPTER XVIII

THE LETTER-WRITER

"How's them war correspondents going on?" inquired Private Smith. "Are they still 'somewhere in the North of France,' or have they left Boulogne? I'm only askin' because I thought I saw a letter of Nobby Clark's in the paper this mornin' signed 'Sister Agnes.'

"This is a soldiers' war all right. Soldier bus-drivers, soldier engine-drivers, soldier mud-larks, an' soldier war correspondents. Before I 'stopped one'* on the Aisne I often used to regret I hadn't any relations to write home to, givin' full particulars of me heroic deeds an' the terrible way I was killin' Germans. It's grand to see the way Tiny White an' Spud Murphy an' other gallant fellers of 'B' Company have been slaughterin' the foe, an' only them that know the true fac's realises how much they've got to thank Nobby Clark who, so to speak, was the originator of the idea for the most interestin' feature in the newspapers.

* "Stop one" is the soldier's descriptive synonym for being wounded—i.e. stopping a bullet.

"I don't say that Nobby Clark foresaw the day when the public would be fed up with such items as:

'On the Lyser there was an artillery duel.
At Alas we have made progress.
In the Allgonne there is nothin' to report.'

"But what Nobby did know was that war correspondents wouldn't be allowed.

"It was when we was in billets on the Marne that Nobby sez one night suddenly:

"'I wonder where Hector is to-night?'

"'Who's Hector?' sez Spud Murphy.

"'Hector,' sez Nobby very deliberate, 'is me young brother.'

"It happened that Sergeant Hasty, the orderly-room sergeant, was billeted with us in the handsome an' commodious barn we was supposed to sleep in.

"Sergeant Hasty is—or was—one of them sharp-faced fellers who do sums in their heads, an' can tell you the date of the Great Fire of London without so much as lookin' at an almanac.

"'Clark,' he sez, 'accordin' to my memory, an' havin' seen all your papers, you haven't got any relations except an uncle.'

"Nobby didn't turn a hair.

"'Hector,' he sez again, 'is me brother, sergeant, an' if I haven't mentioned it, it's because of me family pride. Hector's got two shops of his own....'

"'What sort of shops?' sez Spud.

"'Boot shops,' sez Nobby, 'where you sell boots. Naturally enough, bein' a master man an' highly respected, he don't want the neighbours to know that he has a brother servin' as a common soldier.'

"'That's what I call a snob,' sez the sergeant.

"'That's what other people call him,' sez Nobby, 'only I prefer to call him a bootmaker.'

"Never havin' heard of Nobby's brother I was a bit surprised until Nobby told me that he thought of writin' a letter to him givin' full particulars about the retreat from Mons.

"'The only difficulty is that I don't know his address,' sez Nobby, 'but I'm goin' to get over that in a highly novel way. I'm sendin' the letter to the Editor of the Daily Tribune.'

"That was a bit hot, because it's a court-martial crime to write to the papers, but Nobby had arranged to get over that.

"'I'm sendin' a letter to the Editor,' he sez, an' showed it to me when I was doin' my bit of trench diggin'.

'Dear Sir,—The following letter composed by me is written for my brother, Hector Clark, Esq. Not knowing his address, will you publish same and pay my brother for same when he calls, as same belongs to him, only I haven't got his address? My brother will say, "Please give me the money for my brother's letters," and you will pay the same over. P.S.—My brother will be dressed as a soldier the same as me.— Yours truly, N. Clark.'

"'There's a good many "sames" in that letter,' I sez, 'an' who is your brother, Nobby?'

"'Me an' him are the same,' sez Nobby Clark.

"Nobby was very proud of his grand idea, an' talked to a lot of people about it. All the troops agreed it was fine, except Spud Murphy.

"'It looks to me like daylight robbery an' fraud,' he sez.

"'That's a natural way for you to look at things,' sez Nobby, 'but all honest people will call it "stratagem of war," as the poet says.'

"It was soon after this that letters began arrivin' for the troops—the first mail we had had since we had been in the country—an' a reg'iar epidemic of letter-writin' set in.

"You couldn't walk up the village street where we was billeted without twenty fellers sayin':

"'What's another word for "terrible"? I've used it six times an' it's gettin' monotonous.'

"Sometimes it was 'terrible' an' sometimes it was 'heroic' an' sometimes it was 'undaunted.' but gen'rally it was somethin' about theirselves they was writin'.

"It was about this time when Nobby Clark an' Spud Murphy fell out over a question of money. It appears that Nobby had bought a pair of boots from Spud an' had borrowed ten shillin's on the top of it. Nobby had sworn to pay it back before the regiment left England, an' when he didn't he explained (on the boat comin' across) that his rich uncle had sent him a note sayin' that the money would be forwarded. Naturally, after the letters came, Spud hung round Nobby a lot.

"'It's no good your worryin' me,' sez Nobby. 'Me dear uncle's letter not havin' arrived I can't do anythin' for you.'

"'I don't believe you mean payin' me,' sez Spud.

"'The things you don't believe,' sez Nobby, 'would stock a library.'

"'I suppose you was hopin' I'd "stop one," sneers Spud. 'That's the sort of man you are.'

"'Don't you see I'm busy?' sez Nobby sternly. 'What d'ye mean by wurryin' me when I'm writin' to me dear brother?'

"But Spud wasn't to be put off. There was a rumour that we was goin' to march into Paris, an' he wanted to buy a few things to send home. He got so persistent that Nobby told him all about the letters he was writin' to the Daily Tribune.

"'I'll make lashin's of money,' he sez, 'an' all you've got to do is to be patient.'

"That sort of put Spud in a better temper, an' he said he'd wait.

"Them letters of Nobby was certainly worth money. You've probably seen 'em in print. There was one which began:

'Midnight approaches an' nought can be heard but the sound of a sentry scratchin' his head as he peers fiercely into the night with one hand, an' grasps his rifle firmly with the other, singin' a low melody between his clenched teeth as his sleepin' comrades moan in their sleep thinkin' of home.'

"Letter followed letter in quick succession. Nobby's description of the takin' of Mons, an' his description of the fight at Landrecics, an' Nobby's grand bit about the takin' of the guns at Compiegne are pretty well famous.

'Dear Hector, how can I describe the events of the past week? Words fail me. I cannot describe them. They are indescribable. I will now tell you what happened.'

"'They're mountin' up,' sez Nobby. 'That's four letters I've sent an' I'll bet you they won't pay less than a pound each.'

"Nobby described things he'd seen, an' things he'd heard about, but the most popular letters was them that told of things that nobody had ever heard tell of. It was Nobby who described how him an' another feller was carried off by Zeppelins an' rescued in mid-air by a French aeroplane. It was Nobby who saved the regiment by blowin' up a bridge an' swimmin' across the river carryin' a German prisoner in his teeth,

"When I was sent home I used to buy the Daily Tribune an' read about Nobby's deeds till I was dizzy.

'We have received another vivid letter from Private C of the —chester Regt. (sez the paper), an' we doubt if any of our readers will be able to peruse the followin' story of a British soldier's gallant an' successful attempt to spike a 16-inch German howitzer without feelin' violently ill.'

"I used to get letters from Nobby. He told me that the papers was payin' two pound for each letter, an' that Spud Murphy was worryin' him for money, an' what he was goin' to do to Spud, an' similar gossip.

"Then one day—about a month ago—I got a letter from the Union Jack Club in the Waterloo Road, an' to my surprise it was from Nobby!

"He had come over with an officer of ours who was carryin' despatches, an' was goin' to be in London for three days. I went up to see him—I'd got my sick furlough, an' could walk about quite nicely with a stick.

"'Smithy,' he sez, 'we'll go round to the Daily Tribune office, an' draw my money—at least my brother's money,' he sez, an' then he asked me if I'd seen Spud.

"'Is he home?' I sez.

"'Yes,' sez Nobby, 'rheumatism in the leg,' he sez. 'At least that's what he sez it is.'

"Curiously enough we met a chap of ours in the Strand who'd just seen Spud.

Which way did he go?' sez Nobby interested, and the chap pointed to the Charing Cross end of the Strand.

"'He is the one fellow I don't want to meet,' sez Nobby cheerful. 'We'll go the other.'

"'The fact is,' sez Nobby, 'I owe Spud two pound odd—I tossed him double or quits, an' he won, an' on a joyous day like this, with me treasury chest flowin' with milk an' money, it'd be little less than a disaster to meet anybody I owed two pound to.'

"'Why don't you pay him?' I sez.

"Nobby looks at me pityin'ly.

"'Gettin' wounded has turned your brain, Smithy,' sez he.

"At the office of the Daily Tribune everybody was very decent, an' we was taken up in the lift to one of the editors.

"'So you're Private Clark's other brother, are you?' he sez, an' handed over four pounds. 'There was eight due to you,' he sez, 'but your younger brother called an' collected half.'

"'My younger brother!' sez Nobby faintly.

"'Yes,' sez the editor chap. 'He told me you'd be callin' for the rest in a day or two—here's his receipt.'

"He pulled out a bit of paper.

'Received with deep thanks, £4—'

"An' it was signed—

'Spud Murphy Clark.'

"Nobby came out of the newspaper office in a sort of dream, clutchin' the money in his right hook.

"'Smithy,' he sez in a holler voice, 'which way did that chap say Spud Murphy went?'

"So I told him, an' he called a taxi.

"'Drive toward Charin' Cross,' he sez to the driver, 'an' stop at the first ironmonger's you come to—I want to buy an axe.'"

CHAPTER XIX

THE WEATHER PROPHET

"If you were to ask me," said Smithy, "who's got the quickest brain in the Anchester Regiment, I'd up an' say 'Nobby Clark.' Not because he's a pal of mine, not because him an' me has soldiered together in all parts of the world from Paris to Paardeburg, but because I've sort of stood outside meself an' watched him.

"Lots of people who don't know Nobby think he's unscrupulous. Spud Murphy thinks so, but then he don't know Nobby properly. Tiny White thinks so, but that is only because Tiny an' him fell out over weather prophetin'. The truth about Nobby is that he's a born prophet.

"Tiny always had a hobby of foretellin' the weather. It's easier than tippin' horses, because, so to speak, the field is half-way home before you give your Gran' Twelve o'Clock Final for the Big Race.

"He used to sit at the table with a sheet of paper, a pen and ink, an' an Old Moore's Almanac, an' give predictions that was highly impressive.

"'There's a depression approachin' these isles,' he sez one day, 'an' a hanti-cyclone workin' up from the Azoreys—takin' one thing with another, there ought to be rain in the north-west of Scotland to-morrer.'

"'What about the south-east of Ireland?' sez Nobby.

"'Fog,' sez Tiny prompt. 'Fog an' local thunderstorms.'

"Tiny's predictions never dealt with anywhere nearer than the north of Scotland, so we hardly ever knew for certain if they had come off. He used to tell us they had, but there was nothin' about it in the papers.

"Naturally, we didn't expect to read startlin' headlines like

'Rain at Strathbrassie,'
'Great excitement in Scotland,'

every time Tiny struck a winner.

"Occasionally he'd go farther out, an' once he predicted a terrible storm in the Atlantic.

"'I'm glad I'm not on the sea to-night,' he sez; 'what with that low pressure comin' up from the Azoreys an' the high pressure revolvin' westward from Ireland, they won't half have a time crossin' the Atlantic.'

"We spent two days an' a lot of money buyin' the evenin' an' mornin' papers to see if anything had happened to the mail-boats. The only bit of news we had was that the crossin' had been very smooth, an' that the Carmania had sighted a dead whale.

"'Killed by the storm,' sez Tiny very solemn, 'higher up towards Greenland an' Iceland an' the North Pole,' he sez.

"'Why don't you do a bit o' weather predictin' nearer home?' sez Nobby. 'What's the use of wastin' your talents on the North Pole? Nobody cares if it snows there.'

"But Tiny wouldn't give any predictions nearer home—not unless he were obliged. They tried to get him to deliver a word or two about the weather on the day we played the West Kents in the third round of the Army Cup, but he wouldn't give it till within an hour of the match bein' played, an' even then he was wrong.

"I don't think Nobby took much interest in weather predictin' because, as far as me an' Nobby could see, there was no money in it.

"Tiny went away to the reserve an' was called up for the war. He used to be a very decent chap before what I might term the contaminatin' influence of civilian life got at him. He came back to the Army wearin' spats—an' nothin' gives away a feller worse than spats.

"'Oh, yes,' he sez, very languid, 'I'm dreadfully keen on meteor-ology.'

"'What's her name?' sez Nobby.

"'Meteor-ology,' sez Tiny, 'the science,' he sez, 'of studyin the weather. An' it's goin' to pay me,' he sez.

"Nobby was interested at once.

"It appears that before the Expeditionary Army went out, the Government started a weather department to accompany the Army in the field. It sounds a rum idea, but there is a lot of sense in it.

"Nobby explained it to me afterwards.

"Suppose the General is makin' arrangements for a big battle. He sends for the weather expert.

"'What sort of weather are we goin' to have?' sez the General.

"'Strong westerly breezes, mong general,' sez the weather sergeant.

"'Good!' sez the General. 'Then we'll attack the enemy from the east—they won't smell us comin'.'

"Tiny said that a friend of his in the weather department at Victoria Street had told him all about it. The New Weather Corps was to tell the aeroplanes how long they could stay up.

"'I've put in me name,' sez Tiny, 'an' I dare say I shall be transferred in a day or two. The pay is six shillin's a day—'

"'Say no more, Tiny,' sez Nobby, speakin' with great emotion; 'me an' you will transfer together.'

"'What do you know about the weather?' sez Tiny, very amazed.

"'I've been out in all kinds of it,' sez Nobby.

"The next mornin' Nobby paraded before the adjutant.

"'You want to join the Weather Brigade?' sez the Adjutant, puzzled. 'An' what the devil is the Weather Brigade?'

"So Nobby up an' told him.

"'I've never heard of it,' sez the Adjutant; 'somebody has been pullin' your leg—besides, you know nothin' about the weather.'

"'Sir,' sez Nobby, 'there ain't anythin' about the weather that I don't know.'

"'What sort of an evenin' are we goin' to have?' sez the Adjutant.

"'Variable breezes,' sez Nobby, 'with slight rain in places; fine later; cooler.'

"An' all that Nobby predicted was true," said Smithy in a hushed voice, "just as he said it, it came off.

"The next day the Adjutant sees Nobby goin' across the square and calls him.

"'Your weather prediction was good,' he sez. 'What newspaper did you read it in?'

"'Paper, sir?' sez Nobby surprised. 'I didn't know they had weather predictions in newspapers.'

"'What is the weather going to be like today?' sez the Adjutant.

"'Cloudy, with localshowers,' sez Nobby, 'and cooler.'

"'Daily Telegraph,' sez the Adjutant.

"Nobby saluted.

"'Beg pardon, sir,' he sez, 'the Telegraph sez "warmer."'

"'Go away, Private Clark,' sez the Adjutant, 'before I forget meself.'

"Now the rum thing was that, instead of bein' 'warmer,' as the paper said, it was cooler, and that's where Nobby Clark's reputation as a weather expert started to grow.

"An' it increased after we got to France, because, havin' no newspapers to go on, an' being obliged, so to speak, to depend on his own wonderful powers, the troops could see there was no hanky-panky, an' that Nobby was the genuine weather expert of the 1st Anchesters.

"Tiny White was nothin' to Nobby. Tiny was wild as anythin', but he had to take a second place.

"'What's the weather goin' to be like?' he sneers one mornin'—it was the day we en-motor-'bussed for X—.

"'Fine with thunderstorms,' sez Nobby, 'an' warmer in the evenin'.'

"'You're wrong,' sez Tiny. 'We shall have rain, and it will be cooler.'

"'Noos verongs,' sez Nobby.

"'What's that mean?' sez Tiny.

"'It's a French weather expression,' sez Nobby.

"Tiny was in D Company, an' me an' Nobby was in old historic B, an', as everybody knows, B Company and D Company of the Anchesters are on pretty bad terms.

"It was only natural that D should stand up for Tiny and B for Nobby, an' when we reached the advanced base it wasn't anythin' unusual to see the chaps of D Company diggin' little trenches round their tents to carry off the rain what Tiny said was comin', whilst B Company chaps was hangin' out their washin' to dry because Nobby had predicted 'variable breezes—warmer.'

"One mornin', when there wasn't a cloud in the sky, Tiny got out his prediction, 'Fine and pleasant for the next twenty-four hours,' and it rather looked as if Nobby would have to come into line, or else get himself severely tangled up.

"'Smithy,' he sez, 'I've got to do somethin'—the eyes of the battalion are on me.'

"An' that was a fact. Even the officers was beginnin' to believe in Nobby, and Major Anstruther of D used to bet the Adjutant real money that his man beat Nobby Clark.

"Nobby sat down very serious, an' produced what I might term the most complete weather tip that's ever been issued. He wrote it down on a bit of paper, and Lance-Corporal Tingle of the orderly room made copies of it:

"'There's a heavy depression approachin' from the north, an' a big storm is expected with thunder and lightning. This is one of the biggest storms ever known. It will move in a southerly direction, and will carry everything before it. Warmer an' sultry."

Smithy paused and went on solemnly:

"Don't let anybody tell me that Nobby ain't a prophet. That same day our division was rushed to Mons, and by sunset that there depression from the north struck us—five army corps of it. It was the kind of storm I never want to see again, for it lasted till we was south of the Marne, an' the thunder hasn't stopped yet."

CHAPTER XX

THE INTERPRETER

"In this world," said Private Smith in his most philosophical frame of mind, "nothin' helps a man to overcome what I might term the difficulties of life so much as a good memory an' a knowledge of languages—ahem!"

Smithy and I met in the buffet at the Gare de Lyons. A wounded officer now convalescent was returning from Lyons, and Smithy was to meet him.

"Troops comin' out to France have, naturally enough, a desire to mallum the bat.*

* Tommyesque Hindustani, meaning to "speak" the "language."

"Lots of chaps gave it out, before the regiment left England, that what they didn't know about the French language might, so to speak, be safely left to the General Staff.

"Nobby Clark had a book sent to him by his brother—he bought it cheap in Farringdon Road—called Easy Conversations Fransaze, an' when it come out in orders that officers an' men acquainted with French should hand their names in to the orderly room, Nobby up an' proclaimed himself one of the finest French scholars of the age.

"The Adjutant called Nobby out on parade.

"'I see you've put your name in as an interpreter, Clark?' he sez.

"'Yes, sir,' sez Nobby.

"'Do you speak French?' sez the Adjutant.

"'We, we,' sez Nobby.

"'Avec facilimong?' sez the officer.

"'Nong, nong, mong Capitong,' sez Nobby.

"'I asked you if you spoke it with facility,' sez the Adjutant.

"'No, mong Capitong,' sez Nobby, 'with a book.'

"'Not so much of the "mong Capitong,"' sez the officer.

"Anyway, they didn't take Nobby.

"Well, mobilisation began, an' Nobby, being bitten with the idea of walkin' about in an officer's uniform interpretin', hit on a plan.

"He had an uncle in London, an' every afternoon when he wasn't for duly Nobby went up to town to his uncle's, and, changing into civilian kit, went to Dr. Shlielsteimer's Celebrated School of Languages, an' took a couple of hours' lessons.

"'No good my goin' in uniform,' he told me, 'there's always a lot of girls at them places, an' I don't want to be, so to speak, conspicuous. Girls always run after me,' he sez modest.

"'So should I if I was a girl,' I sez.

"'Would you, Smithy?' he asks quite pleased. 'Why?'

"'Because,' I sez, 'if I was follerin' you about I shouldn't sec your ugly mug,' I sez.

"Anyway for a couple of weeks he toiled an' moiled, an' he gave me a good deal of information about the pen of his aunt an' the books of his father's brother that I'd never had before.

"'I'm making good progress,' he sez very enthusiastic. 'The teacher is a feller named Meyerheim—he's a naturalised Austrian, an' he don't spare any pains.'

"Before the lessons was finished, Meyerheim had gone—had to leave sudden for Austria to see the aunt of his mother, takin' two pens, a pencil, an' the book of Thomas. At least, that's what Nobby said, an' as he told me first in French and then in English, I suppose he'd got all the facts.

"Anyway, Meyerheim was gone, an' Nobby took the last of his lessons from another chap.

"'Twelve bob it cost me, but it's worth every penny,' sez Nobby. 'I can talk French like—well, you wait till we get to France.'

"Well, we mobilised at Aldershot, an' off we hopped.

"I must admit that Nobby made himself understood remarkably well. When we got to Boulogne Nobby went up to the first French soldier he saw, an' sez, 'Polly voo Francay?' an' the French soldier looked a bit staggered, but sez 'We, we.' So there couldn't have been much wrong with his accent.

"And when it came to goin' round the shops buyin' things, nobody understood the language so well as Nobby. If he wanted two apples he'd hold up two fingers, an' say, 'Sieve voo play?' An' when the lady told him how much it was, he'd give her a franc and count the change very careful.

"'How do you know how much she sez?' I asked him once.

"'I don't,' sez Nobby, 'until I've counted the change.'

"Lots o' people who didn't believe that Nobby could speak French at first altered their opinions. We used to be hard up for newspapers, the only ones comin' our way being the papers we got up from Paris, an' the troops used to bring 'em in an' sit round in a circle whilst Nobby translated 'em. Some of the papers was good, an' some was not so good. The one Nobby liked best was a paper called La Vee Parisien. A rare paper for war news that was, an' it gave pictures of patriotic French ladies who'd given all their clothes to the poor. Some people used to say that there was no war news in La Vee Parisien, but that only shows what a fat lot they knew about it.

"Nobby would turn the leaves over very solemn, turnin' his head away so that he couldn't see the pictures, an' by an' by he'd say:

"'Hullo—here's a bit.'

'It is rumoured that another million German recruits are drillin' like mad.'

"'What's "drillin' like mad" in French?' says Spud Murphy, the only suspicious feller in the whole battalion.

"'Drillong au balmè,' says Nobby, quick as lightnin', an' went on readin'.

"There he'd sit for hours translatin' the news. I don't suppose there's a paper in the world with the information of La Vee Parisien.

'It is reported,' reads Nobby, 'that the citizens of Hornsey are gettin' up a testimonial to that gallant hero, Private Spud Murphy, of 1st Anchesters, who is to be engraved on vellum an' bound.'

"'Is that there?' asks Spud incredulously.

"'Do you doubt me word?' sez Nobby.

"'It's very likely,' sez Spud highly gratified. 'My family has lived in Hornsey for years, an' me father has driven the corporation water-cart since 1887—do they say what the testimonial is for?'

"'Yes,' sez Nobby, 'it's owin' to the decrease in crime since you was called up.'

"When the advance started an' we moved up to Mons to that celebrated battle, Nobby found lots of opportunity for speakin' the language. People brought us flowers an' grub, an' the way Nobby kept sayin' 'Mercy, mercy,' was wonderful to hear. What's more, all these French ladies and gentlemen understood him. Two days before the battle we was billeted in the little town of X—. There was four of us chaps billeted in a labourer's cottage, an' the way those people put themselves out for us was wonderful. That night, after we'd had a reg'lar officers' mess dinner, Nobby was sent for. The Adjutant was standin' in the middle of the street talkin' to a French soldier.

"'Clark,' sez the Adjutant, 'you speak French, I understand.'

"'In a sense—yes, sir,' sez Nobby.

"'Well, you can look after this man—he's billeted in your house.'

"So Nobby pointed to the house with his thumb, an' the soldier understandin' the language, went along with him.

"It was a bit of a joke on the Adjutant's part, for this chap spoke English. He'd come up from Charleroi, he said, an' had got cut off from his lot by a party of Uhlans.

"A nice affable feller he was, an' spoke as good English as me an' Nobby.

"'Do you speak French?' he sez to Nobby.

"'Ung petty pair,' sez Nobby, modest.

"'You'll pick it up,' sez the chap. 'I speak English because I was a waiter in London for years.'

"An' then he began to talk about the war an' how he'd left his old folks an' his wife in Amiens, an' how he hated the Germans.

"'When are you chaps movin' to Mons?' he sez, sudden.

"'To-morrow,' sez Nobby.

"As a matter of fact, nobody knew when we was movin' or where, but Nobby is a sort of feller that never likes people to think that he don't know everything.

"'Where's your artillery now?' sez the French soldier.

"'Down the road,' sez Nobby, an' this French feller went on askin' all sorts of questions. He told us his name was De Boosong, or a name that sounded like that.

"Nobby went out soon after, an' me an' the other two chaps in the billet strolled out after a bit, talkin' about the troops an' where they was, an' how many big guns we had. We was lookin' at an ambulance waggon when up came Nobby, and behind him was the Adjutant an' a file of the guard.

"'Take that man,' sez the Adjutant, an' they seized the French soldier.

"'Your name is Meyerheim, an' you are a spy,' sez the Adjutant.

"We made a rapid search of him an' found rough plans with the positions of all the troops from Boulogne to X— marked in ink. Then we took him back to the cottage.

"The Colonel came in, an' another officer, an' they tried him at the table where our supper had been laid.

"'You'll be shot at daybreak,' sez the Colonel.

"The spy looked round at Nobby.

"'I remember you now,' he sez, 'you wore civilian clothes when you come to my class—ah, well!'—he shrugged his shoulders an' walked out between the guard.

"'How did you recognise him, Clark?' sez the Adjutant.

"Nobby looked thoughtful at the ceilin'.

"'By his bad French accent, sir,' he sez.

CHAPTER XXI

NOBBY IN ROMANTIC VEIN

"Nobby Clark wrote a poem of hate once," said Smithy, "an' as it happened before the war, an' was meant for a feller who'd gone away to join the 2nd Battalion in India owin' him money, it probably gave the German poet the idea which he's got all the credit for.

"Off an' on Nobby's been writin' poems for years an' gen'rally they've been successful.

"Often an' often me an' Nobby has had to come a long way round to camp instead of takin' a short cut through the Wigshires' lines, owin' to some little poem what Nobby writ about the Wigshire Regiment's way of playin' football.

"Nobby used to do verses at the front for some of the chaps. They was versus like:

Under the starry sky,
With the shells a burstin' nigh,
I think of you, my lass so true,
As in the mud I lie.

"Nobby has always been handy with his pen an' that's probably why he's always in trouble, for as the poet sez, 'the pen is flightier than the sword.'

"After the shockin' an' outrageous behaviour of the Germans who made me an' Nobby an' about 80,000 other fellers walk all the way from Mons to the Marne without givin' us time to change our boots, there follered a long time of trench work when we had plenty of opportunity for receivin' an' writin' letters. An' this wasn't all.

"Lots of people in England, anxious to do somethin' for the soldiers, were sendin' out mufflers, mittens, chocolate, an' cigarettes—which in addition to bein' highly appreciated was very useful.

"It was a bit of luck—what you received, I mean.

"Spud Murphy got Pilgrim's Progress an' a box of Turkish delight. Big Tony White, who had toothache all the way down, got a box of chocolate, but Nobby, who was born with a set of gold soup ladles in his mouth, got a couple of shirts which was both useful an' ornamental, bein' sky-blue in colour and hand-embroidered.

"But it was the note pinned to the shirts that appealed to Nobby who, as I say, was a born poet. This is what it said:

Whoever you are, whatever you be,
I've made these shirts with care for thee.
So, soldier, kindly write to me.

From Lady Gwendoline FitzMalling,
Knadsley Hall, Knadsley, Kent.

P.S.—Please send the answer inclosed in a letter to my servant Mary Ann Gabbler at above address.'

"'I always thought I should get into society,' sez Nobby.

"'She wouldn't have written it if she knew the shirts was comin' to you,' said Spud Murphy. 'She thought they was goin' to officers—you can tell that by the decorations.'

"'Push off, kill-joy!' sez Nobby. 'Go back to your own bloomin' trench—you're bringin' us bad luck.'

"Certainly the decorations was very fine. When Nobby held up the shirt for the troops to see there was a lion an' a unicorn fightin' for a crown on the chest, a Belgian flag on one sleeve, an' a harp an' a crown on the other.

"'It's more like a drawin'-room carpet than a shirt,' sez Spud.

"'Don't display your ignorance before the young soldiers,' sez Nobby sternly. 'This is a shirt of honour—like you read about. It's the sort of shirt the Archbishop of Canterbury or the Lord Chief Justice wears.'

"'I've never seen one like it,' sez Spud.

"'Poor old Spud!' sez Nobby kindly. 'Havin' spent your life amongst low people who wear cotton shirts, it must be like heaven gettin' into close touch with real class.'

"'I'm goin' to answer that letter,' he sez to me later in the day—'I'll have to make up a real good one.'

"An' he did.

"It started: 'Dear Lady Gwendoline, if you'll excuse the liberty,' and went on:

"'When I received your kind an' welcome letter I was rescuin' a number of comrades from death—'

("'That ain't true,' sez Nobby, 'but they like little realistic an' romantic bits.')

"'My thoughts often turn,' the letter went on, 'to Knadsley Hall, Knadsley, Kent, an' so do the shirts you so kindly sent, which I am wearin' now. How can a lonely soldier who has no friends thank you?'

("'That's romance, too,' sez Nobby.)

"'My history is a sad one,' Nobby wrote. 'Alone in the world—I shall never feel lonely now that I am wearin' your shirts—an orphan, an' my proud spirit crushed by a cruel stepfather....'

"Nobby wrote one of the grandest letters that have ever been written, an' sent it off.

"'I don't suppose she'll write back,' sez Nobby; 'still there have been lots of romantic things happen in the world, an' perhaps....'

"She wrote back all right. The letter was brought up to the fire trench one evenin' an' Nobby read it by candle-light. I saw him makin' happy faces as he read it, but it wasn't till the next mornin' that he showed it to me.

'Dearest!' sez the letter, 'I have not seen your face, but already I know you! Write to me, oh my heart! From Lady Gwendoline FitzMalling, Knadsley Hall, Knadsley, Kent.'

"'This,' sez Nobby, speakin' with great emotion, 'is one of the most romantic, things that's ever happened.'

"It made a rare difference to Nobby, that letter. I never saw the answer he sent to it, but one day when we was in the reserve trenches he told me that he was as good as married.

"'Me an' Gwen will always be glad to see you, Smithy,' he sez. 'We'll send the dogcart down to the station for you, an' you can have your breakfast in bed. In the mornin' I'll be waitin' for you in the rosery, an' we'll have a pipe an' talk over old times.'

"'Yes, me lord,' I sez.

"'Say that again,' sez Nobby, an' I obliged him.

"'I suppose I shall be Lord Clark,' he sez thoughtful. 'Somehow, I always thought I should get on.'

"He had wonderful ideas, had Nobby. He couldn't make up his mind whether he'd breed pigs or horses. We had a long discussion about it one night.

"'I'd breed pigs,' sez Spud Murphy. 'They'll prevent you feelin' lonely.'

"'They'll also remind me of the low people I've had to associate with,' sez Nobby.

"'Don't you ever invite me down to your house,' sez Spud. 'I'm a Socialist.'

"'Reste tronkill,' sez Nobby in French.

"Another letter came from the lady—pages an' pages of it, an' Nobby got haughtier than ever.

"Spud Murphy saw the R.A.M.C. orderly at the collectin' station.

"'You might ask your bloke somethin' for us,' he sez. 'We've had a bet an' we want to decide whether Knadsley Hall is a lunatic asylum or a home for chronic drinkers.'

"Ordinarily Nobby would have resented this, but he only smiled superiorly.

"'Pore feller!' he sez; 'such lowness!'

"The R.A.M.C. chap asked his officer, an' the doctor surprised Spud by sayin' that Knadsley Hall was the home of the Earl of Knadsley, an' that Lady Gwendoline was his only daughter.

"'Me last hopes gone,' sez Spud bitterly.

"There wasn't a lot of time for confidences an' discussions after that. Von Kluck an' his friends got very busy, an' we spent most of our time countin' the shells that burst over our trench an' shootin' back the infantry attacks that follered.

"The story got out about Nobby an' his lady, an' the amount of attention our line created was truly astoundin'. Every time a shell burst over our trench, the chaps in the other trenches said: 'There goes the heir to Knadsley Hall,' or 'Another empty chair in the House of Lords.'

"Marchin' back through the darkness at night to our billets, fellers of other regiments would come to the side of the road an' ask: 'Is little Lord Fauntleroy still alive?' until Nobby began to know what it felt like to be famous.

"'I don't suppose her parents know anythin' about it yet,' sez Nobby one day. 'She's keepin' it dark—you can see that by the way she has her letters addressed to her servant.'

"Nobby gave me an idea how Gwen would break the news.

"The family would be sittin' at breakfast in the parlour one mornin' (accordin' to Nobby), an' Lady Gwen, very pale an' very tall, would get up, an' washin' her hands in the silver rose-bowl in the centre of the table, would say:

"'Papa—may I see you in the picture gallery?'

"An' the old lord would say: 'Certainly, child,' an' then she'd throw herself in his arms weepin' and confess the truth.

"'What!' sez the old lord, 'a private soldier—never!'

"'He is a hero, papa,' sobs Lady Gwen.

"'I'll have no heroes in my family,' sez the old lord. 'Go to your room in the north tower—you are no daughter of mine.'

"But by an' by he'd relent, an' the old bells of Knadsley Parish Church would ring out the glad tidin's.

"'An' then,' sez Nobby, 'I'll turn up one day with me eye in a sling, an' people will take the horses out of the carriage and draw me up to the Hall.'

"'The only bit I believe about that,' sez Spud, 'is that you'll turn up with your eye in a sling—but it will be after you've made your call.'

"There was lots of letters to an' fro, an' I didn't see 'em all. Just before Christmas Nobby had a grand idea.

"'I'll write direct to her,' he sez, 'a very gentlemanly letter that she can show to her people—it'll break the ice,' he sez.

"So one day when the battalion was restin' near Armentières, Nobby did up a fine letter:

'Dear Friend (it went), weather-worn and scarred by war, water, an' worry, I take my pen in my hand to write to you. As I sit here in the trench writin' on a drum by the light of burstin' shells, me mind goes back to the two shirts which I am still wearin'. How can I thank you for your kindness an' how can I thank Mary Ann Gabbler for so kindly givin' you my letters? And how can I thank your dear father the Earl for gettin' the home together, an' how can I thank your mother the Earless for makin' me welcome as I'm sure she will, for she has a beautiful face accordin' to the papers...

"There was a lot more like this.

"'I mention 'em all,' sez Nobby. 'You can't be too careful. Perhaps her servant knows some of the old Earl's secrets an' will be able to put in a word for me.'

"Accordin' to Nobby, Mary Ann might be in a position to say to the Earl: 'Either Mr. Clark marries Lady Gwen or I tell the story of the Red Room an' all that happened on the fatal night of August 22nd, 1876.'

"Nobby hadn't long to wait for an answer. It came one mornin' an' he was very silent. It was two days before he showed me. The letter was short an' written in a different hand to the letters he had been in the habit of receivin':

'Lady Gwendoline FitzMalling presents her compliments to Private Clark and begs to inform him that she is wholly ignorant as to his references re shirts. She gathers that her maid Mary Ann Gabbler, who is a stupid and romantic girl, has been carrying on a correspondence with Private Clark in her (Lady Gwendoline's) name. Mary Ann Gabbler has in consequence been dismissed from her service, and her present address is Polcy Court, New Cut, whither Private Clark should address all future correspondence.'

"Nobby was a bit cut up at first, but then he brightened.

"'These what I might term unequal marriages never turn out well,' he sez, 'an' if anybody asks you, Smithy, you might say that I've broke off my engagement—tell 'em me parents objected,' he sez."

Edgar Wallace – A Short Biography

Richard Horatio Edgar Wallace was born on the 1st April 1875 at 7 Ashburnham Grove, Greenwich. His mother, Mary Jane "Polly" Richards was born into an Irish Catholic family in Liverpool in 1843 and had worked in theatres, both as an actress in bit-parts and as a stagehand and usherette, until she married a Merchant Navy Captain, Joseph Richards, in 1867. He too had been born into an Irish Catholic family in Liverpool. His father had also been a Captain in the Merchant Navy, and his mother's family had a marine background. Mary was eight months pregnant with Joseph's child when he died at sea, and it was once the child had been born that she first turned to the stage, taking the stage name Polly Richards.

She joined the Marriott family theatre troupe in 1872. It was managed by Mrs. Alice Edgar, Richard Edgar, Grace Edgar, Adeline Edgar and Richard Horatio Edgar, Wallace's father. In late 1874 Mary and Richard Horatio Edgar had a brief sexual encounter at the party following a successful show, and she fell pregnant. Worried about the scandal which would ensue and fearing that she might forever lose her job at the troupe, she fabricated an obligation in Greenwich would detain her there for at least six months. She lived in a room in the boarding house on Ashburnham Grove until her son, Edgar, was born. She had already made preparations through her midwife for a couple to foster the child, and when Edgar was born the midwife presented her with Mrs Freeman. Her husband was a fishmonger at Billingsgate market and she already had ten children. She was happy to foster the child and for Polly to make frequent visits to see him in exchange for a small sum of money which Polly made from her work in the theatre troupe.

Wallace was now known as Richard Horatio Edgar Freeman, taking his father's forenames and his foster family's surname. Broadly speaking his childhood was a happy one. The Freemans looked after him lovingly and he had good friendships with his foster siblings, particularly Clara Freeman, twenty years his senior, who often looked after him as a child. After a few years Polly's finances tightened and she was no longer in a position to afford the fee she had been paying the Freemans. However, they had grown to love the young Wallace and opted to adopt him in order to keep him out of the workhouse. Polly could no longer visit him. George Freeman was keen to ensure that he had equal opportunities and did all he could to secure him an education at St. Alfege with St. Peter's, a Peckham boarding school. Despite his adoptive father's efforts, though, Wallace left the school aged twelve for truancy.

Instead he went to work and by the time he was fourteen or fifteen he had experience selling newspapers at Ludgate Circus, near Fleet Street, as a worker in a rubber factory, as a shoe shop assistant, as a milk delivery boy and as a ship's cook. He stole from the milk company which resulted in his dismissal, and in 1894 was engaged to a local girl from Deptford named Edith Anstree, though he broke this off and instead joined the Infantry. He adopted the name Edgar Wallace which he took from Lew Wallace, the author of *Ben-Hur*, and his medical record records a diminutive 33" chest and a stunted growth. his first posting was with the West Kent Regiment in South Africa in 1896, though he did not enjoy military life, arranging to be transferred to the Royal Army Medical Corps. Though this was a less strenuous job, it was also significantly less pleasant and so he again transferred to the Press Corps, which he found suited him far better.

He was in Cape Town in 1898 where he met Rudyard Kipling and was inspired to begin writing and publishing poetry and songs. His first collection of ballads, *The Mission that Failed!* and was enough of a success that in 1899 he paid his way out of the armed forces in order to turn to writing full time. His first work was as a war correspondent for Reuters who kept him in Africa to cover the Boer War, and then for the Daily Mail in 1900 and various other periodicals after that. It was while he was in South Africa that he met and married Ivy Maude Caldecott, who was 21 when they married in 1901, despite her Wesleyan missionary father's strong opposition to the union, for several reasons, one of which was that Wallace's writing was not turning quite the profit he had expected it would. *War and Other Poems* and *Writ in Barracks,* both published in 1900, had not proved as popular as his first collection. Eleanor Clare Hellier Wallace, their first child, died of meningitis in 1903 and, in rather deep debt, they returned to London. Wallace used his contacts with the Daily Mail to get work with them in London, electing to write detective novels as a means of making quick money.

Wallace met Polly, his birth mother, in 1903. He didn't remember her from his childhood as he had been too young when she became unable to visit, so it was as though they were meeting for the first time.

She was sixty years old and terminally ill, living in abject poverty. She had come to Wallace seeking financial support, but he turned her away. She died in the Bradford Infirmary later that year. In 1904 he and Ivy had a son, Bryan. He was still writing and had completed his first thriller, *The Four Just Men*. Since nobody would publish it he resorted to setting up his own publishing company which he called Tallis Press and he published a serialised version of *The Four Just Men* in 1905. He received promotional assistance from the Daily Mail in which he ran a competition for entrants to guess the method of murder in the final chapter, with a prize of £1,000 for a correct guess. Although the paper's proprietor, Lord Alfred Harmsworth, refused Wallace the £1,000 prize money, Wallace persisted and went ahead with the competition, recklessly advertising on billboards and buses all over the country, hoping to expand his advertisements across the Empire. His worried colleagues at the Daily Mail managed to convince him to lower the prize money to £500, split into a first prize of £250, a second prize of £200 and a third of £50, but with the total cost of his advertisements nearing £2,000 he would need to sell £2,500 worth of copies before he could see any profit. He was confident that this could be achieved in just three months.

Though he had remarkable enthusiasm, it became clear that his managerial skills left a lot to be desired. It soon emerged that nowhere in the competition terms and conditions had he included a clause limiting the competition to one single winner; instead, any entrant with a winning answer was entitled to their corresponding prize money. Thus, if ten entrants guessed the first prize answer, the competition was obliged to pay each entrant £250. This error was only noticed after the competition had been closed and the solution had been printed in the final installment of the novel, meaning that not only was there no opportunity to write his way out of enormous financial obligation, but the entrants who had guessed correctly would by now have read the final chapter and know they had done so. £250 was an enormous amount of money to the average Edwardian family and those entitled to it were likely to make a lot of noise if they didn't receive their money. Despite this, Wallace's fist instinct was to attempt to ignore the issue entirely, even as he discovered that he initial calculations had been dramatically over-enthusiastic and it would take nearer to two years of continuous sales to break even at the initial cost of £2,500, let alone the new figure which included every correct guesser. Compounding the problem even further was the awful realisation that as sales continued throughout the initial three month period and Wallace approached the £2,500 break-even figure, new readers were still eligible to enter and guess correctly. Though it is unknown how much he eventually owed his readers, Lord Harmsworth found himself having to loan over £5,000 in order to protect the reputation of the newspaper, since 1906 had come around and there still hadn't been a list printed of all prize-winners. It was less a charitable act than one of a man anxious that the failure would reflect ill on his own paper. Wallace filed for bankruptcy shortly thereafter and as a token gesture to his creditors sold the rights to the novel to Sir George Newnes, a publisher and editor, for £75. In the midst of this chaos though, Wallace managed to write and published *Smithy*, which would become the first of a series of *Smithy* novels.

Following this fiascos Wallace was dismissed from the Daily Mail in 1907 when inaccuracies which were found in his reporting, resulting in libel cases being brought against the paper. That year he became the first reporter to be fired from the Daily Mail and was his awful reputation prevented him from finding work at any other papers. Despite all this, though, he travelled to the Congo Free State later that year and reported on the criminal treatment of the Congolese people by King Leopold II of Belgium and the Belgian rubber companies. Up to fifteen million Congolese were killed in various atrocities, and Wallace was asked to serialise stories based on his experiences for her penny magazine *Weekly Tale-Teller*. He and Ivy had another daughter, named Patricia, in 1908. Though his new work for *Weekly Tale-Teller* was bringing in some money, their financial situation was still dire and Ivy was occasionally forced to sell off her jewellery and possessions in order to pay for food. In 1911 his Congolese stories were published in a collection called *Sanders of the River*, which quickly became a bestseller. He would publish eleven more such collections featuring a total of 102 stories of adventure and tribal life set on the river Congo.

From 1908 he started to enjoy a revival of both his success and his reputation. The majority of his initial writing he sold outright in order to make money as quickly as possible and placate his creditors in the United Kingdom and South Africa, but as his success saw the reestablishment of his reputation he began to find work once again as a journalist, beginning in horse racing for the *Week-End*, the *Evening News* and then as an editor for the *Week-End Racing Supplement*. Following this success he started his own racing papers, *Bibury's* and *R. E. Walton's Weekly*, eventually buying his own racehorses and losing thousands gambling. His success was insufficient to support his newly extravagant lifestyle and his marriage began to fail in the light of his financial irresponsibility. He and Ivy had their last child together, Michael Blair Wallace, in 1916, and she filed for divorce in 1918 moving to Tunbridge Wells with her children.

Wallace began to fall for his secretary Ethel Violet King and they married in 1921, having a child, Penelope Wallace, in 1923, who would herself go on to become a successful crime writer. Wallace now began to take his career as a fiction writer more seriously, signing with Hodder and Stoughton in 1921. He now began to organize his contracts more carefully, arranging for royalties and properly organized promotions, run by people more business-minded than himself. He was marketed as the 'King of Thrillers' and they gave him the trademark image of a trilby, a cigarette holder and a yellow Rolls Royce. He was truly prolific, capable not only of producing a 70,000 word novel in three days but of doing three novels in a row in such a manner. His publishers signed off on almost everything he wrote as soon as he turned it in, estimating that by 1928 one in four books being read at any time was written by Wallace, for alongside his famous thrillers he wrote variously in other genres, including but not limited to science fiction, non-fiction accounts of WWI which amounted to ten volumes and screen plays. Eventually he would reach the remarkable total of 170 novels, 18 stage plays and 957 short stories.

Wallace became chairman of the Press Club which to this day holds an annual Edgar Wallace Award, rewarding 'excellence in writing'. In 1923 he broadcasted a report on the Epsom Derby horse race for the British Broadcasting Company, making him the first ever radio sports correspondent. His ex-wife Ivy had suffered from breast cancer between 1923-1924, and it eventually killed her in 1926 despite a successful operation to remove a tumour the year before. He wrote the essay "The Canker in our Midst" in 1926 which dealt, aggressively and controversially, with the problem of paedophilia in show business, describing how children were unwittingly left open to sexual abuse, and linking paedophilia with homosexuality. Its tone has been described as "intolerant, blustering, kick-the-blighters-down-the-stairs". He was appointed chairman of the British Lion Film Corporation on the back of the success of *The Ringer* and on the agreement that he give British Lion first choice on all his future work. This contract gave him an annual salary and a large amount of stock with the company, along with a stipend on all British Lion production of his work and 10% of their annual profits. This extraordinary contract gave him annual earnings by 1929 of almost £50,000, or almost £2 million in 2014.

He now became an active figure in politics, entering the 1931 general election as a Liberal contestant in Blackpool, rejecting the current government in favour of free trade. He lost the election by over 33,000 votes and went to America in late 1931, once again deeply in debt after buying the *Sunday News* which closed six months later. In America he quickly found work as a script doctor for RKO Pictures, enjoying early success with the 1932 adaptation of *The Hound of the Baskervilles*. This success, along with that of the play *The Green Pack*, established his reputation in America and he was able to see his own work adapted for film, beginning with *The Four Just Men*. His most successful theatrical work, *On The Spot*, which explores the life of Al Capone, has been described as "arguably, in construction, dialogue, action, plot and resolution, still one of the finest and purest of 20th-century melodramas". These successes led to his assignation on RKO's "gorilla picture" which would become famous as King Kong in 1933.

He worked on the first draft though he was beginning to experience severe headaches which brought about a diagnosis of diabetes. Despite taking medication to address his condition, it deteriorated in a matter of days. His wife booked him passage home but soon heard that he had entered a coma and died of his condition and double pneumonia on the 7th of February 1932 in North Maple Drive, Beverly Hills. In his honour the bell at St. Bride's church on Fleet Street tolled for the duration of the morning while the flags flew at half-mast. He was buried near his home in England at Chalklands, Bourne End, in Buckinghamshire. Once again, at the time of his death he was in severe debt, mostly to racing bookkeepers, though these debts were settled within two years thanks to the enormous royalties his estate continued to receive from his contracts. His writing has been translated into 29 languages, and is considered one of the most important bodies of Colonial writing.

Edgar Wallace – A Concise Bibliography

African Novels
Sanders of the River (1911)
The People of the River (1911)
The River of Stars (1913)
Bosambo of the River (1914)
Bones (1915)
The Keepers of the King's Peace (1917)
Lieutenant Bones (1918)
Bones in London (1921)
Sandi the Kingmaker (1922)
Bones of the River (1923)
Sanders (1926)
Again Sanders (1928)

Four Just Men (Series)
The Four Just Men (1905)
The Council of Justice (1908)
The Just Men of Cordova (1917)
The Law of the Four Just Men (US title: Again the Three Just Men) (1921)
The Three Just Men (1926)
Again the Three Just Men (US title: The Law of the Three Just Men) (1929) a.k.a. Again the Three

Mr. J. G. Reeder (Series)
Room 13 (1924)
The Mind of Mr. J. G. Reeder (US title: The Murder Book of Mr. J. G. Reeder) (1925)
Terror Keep (1927)
Red Aces (1929)[27]
The Guv'nor and Other Short Stories (US title: Mr. Reeder Returns) (1932)

Detective Sgt. (Inspector) Elk series

The Nine Bears or The Other Man or The Cheaters (1910)
revised as Silinski - Master Criminal (1930)
The Fellowship of the Frog (1925)
The Joker or The Colossus (1926)
The Twister (1928)
The India-Rubber Men (1929)
White Face (1930)

Educated Evans (Series)
Educated Evans (1924)
More Educated Evans (1926)
Good Evans (1927)

Smithy (Series)
Smithy (1905)
Smithy Abroad (1909)
Smithy and The Hun (1915)
Nobby or Smithy's Friend Nobby (1916)

Crime Novels
Angel Esquire (1908)
The Fourth Plague or Red Hand (1913)
Grey Timothy or Pallard the Punter (1913)
The Man Who Bought London (1915)
The Melody of Death (1915)
A Debt Discharged (1916)
The Tomb of T'Sin (1916)
The Secret House (1917)
The Clue of the Twisted Candle (1918)
Down under Donovan (1918)
The Man Who Knew (1918)
The Strange Lapses of Larry Loman (1918)
The Green Rust (1919)
Kate Plus Ten (1919)
The Daffodil Mystery or The Daffodil Murder (1920)
Jack O'Judgment (1920)
The Angel of Terror or The Destroying Angel (1922)
The Crimson Circle (1922)
Mr. Justice Maxwell or Take-A-Chance Anderson(1922)
The Valley of Ghosts (1922)
Captains of Souls (1923)
The Clue of the New Pin (1923)
The Green Archer (1923)
The Missing Million (1923)
The Dark Eyes of London or The Croakers (1924)
Double Dan or Diana of Kara-Kara (US Title) (1924)
The Face in the Night or The Diamond Men or The Ragged Princess (1924)
The Sinister Man (1924)

The Three Oak Mystery (1924)
The Blue Hand or Beyond Recall (1925)
The Daughters of the Night (1925)
The Gaunt Stranger or Police Work (1925) revised as The Ringer (1926)
A King by Night (1925)
The Strange Countess (1925)
The Avenger or The Hairy Arm (1926)
'The Black Abbot (1926)
The Day of Uniting (1926)
The Door with Seven Locks (1926)
The Man from Morocco or Souls In Shadows or The Black (US Title) (1926)
The Million Dollar Story (1926)
The Northing Tramp or The Tramp (1926)
Penelope of the Polyantha (1926)
The Square Emerald or The Woman (1926)
The Terrible People or The Gallows' Hand (1926)
We Shall See! or The Gaol-Breakers (US Title) (1926)
The Yellow Snake or The Black Tenth (1926)
Big Foot (1927)
The Feathered Serpent or Inspector Wade or Inspector Wade and the Feathered Serpent (1927)
Flat 2 (1927)
The Forger or The Counterfeiter (1927)
Terror Keep (1927)
The Hand of Power or The Proud Sons of Ragusa (1927)
The Man Who Was Nobody (1927)
Number Six (1927)
The Squeaker or The Sign of the Leopard or The Squealer (US Title) (1927)
The Traitor's Gate (1927)
The Double (1928)
The Flying Squad (1928)
The Gunner or Gunman's Bluff (US Title) (1928)
Four Square Jane or The Fourth Square (1929)
The Golden Hades or Stamped In Gold or The Sinister Yellow Sign (1929)
The Green Ribbon (1929)
The Calendar (1930)
The Clue of the Silver Key or The Silver Key (1930)
The Lady of Ascot (1930)
The Devil Man or Sinister Street or Silver Steel
or The Life and Death of Charles Peace (1931)
The Man at the Carlton or The Mystery of Mary Grier (1931)
The Coat of Arms or The Arranways Mystery (1931)
On the Spot: Violence and Murder in Chicago (1931)
When the Gangs Came to London or Scotland Yard's Yankee Dick
or The Gangsters Come To London (1932)
The Frightened Lady or The Case of the Frightened Lady or Criminal At Large (1933)
The Green Pack (1933)
The Man Who Changed His Name (1935)
The Mouthpiece (1935)

Smoky Cell (1935)
The Table (1936)
Sanctuary Island (1936)

Other Novels
Captain Tatham of Tatham Island or Eve's Island or The Island of Galloping Gold (1909)
The Duke in the Suburbs (1909)
Private Selby (1912)
"1925" - The Story of a Fatal Peace (1915)
Those Folk of Bulboro (1918)
The Book of all Power (1921)
Flying Fifty-five (1922)
The Books of Bart (1923)
Barbara on Her Own (1926)

Poetry Collections
The Mission That Failed (1898)
War and Other Poems (1900)
Writ In Barracks (1900)

Non-Fiction
Unofficial Despatches of the Anglo-Boer War (1901)
Famous Scottish Regiments (1914)
Field Marshal Sir John French (1914)
Heroes All: Gallant Deeds of the War (1914)
The Standard History of the War – Volumes 1 – 4 (1914)
Kitchener's Army and the Territorial Forces:
The Full Story of a Great Achievement (1915)
Vol. 2-4. War of the Nations (1915)
Vol. 5-7. War of the Nations (1916)
Vol. 8-9. War of the Nations (1917)
Famous Men and Battles of the British Empire (1917)
Tam of the Scouts (1918)
The Real Shell-Man: The Story of Chetwynd of Chilwell (1919)
People or Edgar Wallace by Himself(1926)
The Trial of Patrick Herbert Mahon (1928)
My Hollywood Diary (1932)

Screenplays
King Kong (1932, first draft of original screenplay, 110 pages) While the script was not used in its entirety, much of it was retained for the final screenplay.
The Hound of the Baskervilles (1932, British film)
The Squeaker (1930, British film)
Prince Gabby (1929, British film)
Mark of the Frog (1928, American film)
The Valley of Ghosts (192

Short Story Collections

The Admirable Carfew (1914)
The Adventure of Heine (1917)
Tam O' the Scouts (1918)
The Fighting Scouts (1919)
Chick (1923)
The Black Avons (1925)
The Brigand (1927)
The Mixer (1927)
This England (1927)
The Orator (1928)
The Thief in the Night (1928)
Elegant Edward (1928)
The Lone House Mystery and Other Stories (1929)
The Governor of Chi-Foo (1929)
Again the Ringer The Ringer Returns (US Title) (1929)
The Big Four or Crooks of Society (1929)
The Black or Blackmailers I Have Foiled (1929)
The Cat-Burglar (1929)
Circumstantial Evidence (1929)
Fighting Snub Reilly (1929)
For Information Received (1929)
Forty-Eight Short Stories (1929)
Planetoid 127 and The Sweizer Pump (1929)
The Ghost of Down Hill & The Queen of Sheba's Belt (1929)
The Iron Grip (1929)
The Lady of Little Hell (1929)
The Little Green Man (1929)
The Prison-Breakers (1929)
The Reporter (1929)
Killer Kay (1930)
Mrs William Jones and Bill (1930)
Forty Eight Short-Stories (1930)
The Stretelli Case and Other Mystery Stories (1930)
The Terror (1930)
The Lady Called Nita (1930)
Sergeant Sir Peter or Sergeant Dunn, C.I.D. (1932)
The Scotland Yard Book of Edgar Wallace (1932)
The Steward (1932)
Nig-Nog and other humorous stories (1934)
The Last Adventure (1934)
The Woman From the East (1934) Co-written By Robert George Curtis
The Edgar Wallace Reader of Mystery and Adventure (1943)
The Undisclosed Client (1963)

Other
King Kong, with Draycott M. Dell, (1933), 28 October 1933 Cinema Weekly

Plays

An African Millionaire (1904)
The Forest of Happy Dreams (1910)
Dolly Cutting Herself (1911)
The Manager's Dream (1914)
M'Lady (1921)
Double Dan (1926)
The Mystery of room 45 (1926)
A Perfect Gentleman (1927)
The Terror (1927)
Traitors Gate (1927)
The Lad (1928)
The Man Who Changed His Name (1928)
The Squeaker (1928)
The Calendar (1929)
Persons Unknown (1929)
The Ringer (1929)
The Mouthpiece (1930)
On the Spot (1930)
Smoky Cell (1930)
The Squeaker (1930)
To Oblige A Lady (1930)
The Case of the Frightened Lady (1931)
The Old Man (1931)
The Green Pack (1932)
The Table (1932)